LEARNING FROM LOVE

BOOK TWO

JESSICA DANIELLE

To my gal pals, Paige and Michelle. Thanks for the support and encouragement.

To my readers, while it's a small group for now. I thank you taking a chance and reading my work.

ALSO BY JESSICA DANIELLE

Learning To Love Again

Learning From Love

FOREWORD

Hi! In an effort to ensure that I do not upset sensitive readers, I am including content warnings for this book to let you know what is in the story to make sure certain readers are not triggered by the content. If I have missed something in my list, please contact me and let me know and I will update the list.

The following things are referenced in the story that you are about to read:

- Discussion of previous abusive relationship
- Mentions of anxiety and PTSD

ONE

The last thing that Willow remembered was guns, shouting, and the burning sensation all over her body as she fell to the ground—and then hearing other pops of the gun before passing out.

Willow opened her eyes slowly, feeling groggy as she looked around the room she was lying in. White walls surrounded her and the beeping next to her head. And the smell of disinfectant was heavy in the air. She moved her right hand and saw an IV line in her arm. She felt like her head was splitting in two as she looked in the door's direction and saw a nurse opening the door.

The woman was wearing flowery printed scrubs, walking into the room, wheeling in a computer on a stand to update Willow's chart. Her eyes looking over the monitor and copy down the numbers into the chart.

"Glad that you are awake, finally. Some people were worried about you," the woman mentioned, who had Willow smiling.

"I take it I have visitors that have been waiting impatiently?" Willow asked, knowing that Amanda would be the one that would annoy the hospital staff about giving more updates until she could come back into the room. Then another thought came to mind; the last she saw of Micheal was when he also landed on the ground next to her.

"Where's Micheal? I know they must've brought him into the hospital with me?" She asked, her fleeting feeling of happiness about her friend annoying the hospital staff now gone and replaced with worry about her boyfriend's status. As she tried to sit up in bed despite the pain that was radiating all over her body. And feeling the IV tug at her arm before the nurse came over and settled Willow down.

"He could be on the same floor. I'll check and see where he is. Mind you, I can only tell you so much with HIPPA laws" the nurse warned as she looked up from the computer.

"Anything you need before I go? I know the doctor that operated on you to remove the bullets will be in here sometime today to give you an update," the woman asked as Willow shook her head.

"I think just water would be ok,"Willow commented as the nurse nodded.

"Want me to tell the people that have been waiting that you are awake or tell them later?" the nurse asked as Willow smiled.

"Oh, if you don't and my friend finds out that I left them waiting while I was awake, I'll get a lecture. So might as well tell them to come on down," Willow said as the nurse smiled, shaking her head as she wheeled the computer out with her before closing the door to Willow's room. Leaving Willow by herself and just with her thoughts; That went from how long her friend waited to see her. Then to think about how Micheal was faring.

The door to the hospital room opening halted those thoughts Willow was having as her best friend, Amanda, stormed in. Willow saw the relief on her face when she caught eye contact with her.

"Oh, thank god, I thought I was going to have to either pay someone off or do something more drastic to get information about how you were doing," Amanda said as she went to take the chair that was next to Willow's bed.

"Oh, I'm told the nurse that was in here the same thing and that I would get a lecture if you weren't told right away that I was awake. So how is everyone else fairing?" Willow asked as Amanda took hold of Willow's left hand that didn't have the IV running out of it.

"Hey, I should ask you that question, and here you're wondering how everyone else is doing. You were the one that got shot and almost died, along with Micheal. We've all been worried, anxiously waiting for updates since we followed the ambulances to the hospital after we showed up at Micheal's house, Willow. So I'm going to ask you, how are you doing?" Amanda said as she squeezed Willow's hand.

"Groggy as hell, and everything hurts. But I think they have me on a morphine drip so it could be worse," Willow said as she heard shuffling outside the hospital room.

"Did you have them wait outside so you could see me first?" Willow asked, trying not to laugh at the fact that Amanda probably put her foot down to Micheal's best friends and coworkers, Eric and Tommy.

"Well, you're my best friend first. We've known each other longer, so I think getting a couple of minutes before the troops come marching in is kinda fair, don't you think?" Amanda questioned rhetorically as Willow laughed just for a second before wincing at the pain that action caused throughout her body. With Amanda's face changing to worry all over it.

"No, no, I'm fine. Now I know, laughing isn't on the agenda for a while with this pain. Which I doubt anyone is going to consider anyway and try to make me laugh." Willow said as she squeezed Amanda's hand and watched her friend roll her dark brown eyes.

"Well, I'm glad to know that despite everything, you haven't lost your sense of humor," Amanda said as the door to the hospital room opened, and Eric and Tommy walked in the door. Amanda whipped her head around to look at the two men that had entered the room, narrowing her eyes at them.

"Didn't I say that I needed time with her alone? Yes, you guys are friends too, but we have been friends for longer. I'll let you know when we are done talking," Amanda said, as Eric and Tommy both rolled their eyes at her—causing Willow to laugh at their lack of response to Amanda's question and demand that they leave.

"Oh, don't you start," Amanda said as she leaned close to Willow. Willow chuckled as she looked up at her friend.

"I see you haven't decided yet? I don't blame you. That's a hard choice," Willow joked as Amanda gritted her teeth.

"Fine, make all the comments you want. Nothing is going on. We are all worried about both of you. That's the only thing that's been going on," Amanda said. She stepped away from Willow. Making Willow think her friend wasn't telling her something, holding back on details as her friend stepped back. She was giving more room for Eric and Tommy to stand closer to Willow.

"She's right, you know. We have worried about you guys ever since we came to the hospital. Then when Micheal woke up from his surgery before you and everything. The healing is different, but from what I heard Micheal say, you got more of it than he did." Eric said as Tommy nodded along in agreement.

"Wait, Micheal is awake? I asked the nurse to give me an update on where he was in the hospital. Have you talked to him? How is he doing?" Willow rattled off as Eric and Tommy looked at each other, smiling, then back at Willow.

"Funny, he's going to be asking the same questions when we go back to his room. When the nurse came to get Amanda to let her know you were awake, he demanded we go for him and get the full report on you." Tommy commented.

"Of course, he has the same questions as I do about him. I'm surprised we've made it here. Which speaking of how is Evan? He was there for some of it, and Andrew and that girl, Carmen, let him go." Willow asked as Eric, Tommy, and Amanda all shared a knowing look between each other.

"He got back with us as we were waiting in the car. He told us what happened, and we drove up after the aftermath while you guys were being put in ambulances. We tried to distance him from it, but he might've seen some things. Which we already know Pam is going to go off on Micheal for. Still waiting for her to show up since I called her personally so she could pick up Evan since it's so late," Eric explained, as the monitor that Willow was connected to started beeping as she tried to take calming breaths to get the sound to stop.

"This whole situation wasn't any of your faults at all. It is more my fault. If Pam has something to say, please have her come to my room to explain the situation to her. This incident isn't Micheal's fault at all," Willow said as Eric and Tommy nodded.

"We are going to stay until Pam comes to pick up Evan. If you need anything, let us know. We'll probably be back tomorrow to visit," Tommy said, taking ahold of Willow's left hand and squeezing it before stepping away as Eric enveloped Willow in a gentle hug. Before stepping away and both leaving the room, which just left Amanda and Willow alone.

Amanda walked the couple of steps to be back to Willow's side, squeezing her hand. "You know this isn't your fault at all. If anyone holds the blame, it should be me. It's my fault this happened," Amanda said as Willow looked up at her with sad eyes; Amanda cleared her throat and stepped away from her.

"I'm just going to leave. Give you time to rest. I'll see you tomorrow," Amanda said as she rushed out of the room, Willow noting that Amanda seemed to have wiped her fingers underneath her eyes as she left the hospital room and closed the door behind her.

Two

Closing the door to Willow's hospital room and leaning against it. Amanda let out a breath, feeling some of the tension leaving her body. She looked to her left and saw Tommy and Eric standing next to the door, waiting for her. Both looked at her, concerned. She felt tears well up in her eyes at what she told Willow.

"It's my fault. All of it is my fault. Willow and Micheal getting attacked wouldn't have happened if it wasn't for me. I should've known, but I didn't see it," Amanda said quietly as she looked over at Eric and Tommy.

"What are you talking about? Andrew was the one that orchestrated this entire thing. That's not your fault," Eric said as he placed his hand on her shoulder.

"Oh, I know that. But I was the reason that Andrew and Willow met each other. If my radar had been up, maybe these past years wouldn't have happened," Amanda said as she sighed.

"I met Andrew first, at my job. I was restocking a section, and in my peripheral, I saw someone standing next to the door, and I moved to let them get whatever they needed. And it was

Andrew. He was the one. He smiled at me. I thought it was cute. But now all I can think is that Willow, I could have been Willow if I didn't tell him I wasn't interested when he tried to come onto me. I stupidly gave Willow's number to him. I could have been Willow. Her laying in that hospital bed, that could have been me if I showed even the slightest bit of interest."

"Then came the dating, and I met him up at the apartment. I mentioned running into him at the grocery store, and he tried to fluff it off when I mentioned I saw him trying to do the same move on other women in the produce section when I was going around restocking sections. It seemed like I was the only one to take the bait, essentially. Even if I gave Willow's Number out to him, he got what he wanted. Willow was innocent. She saw him for how he presented himself to her. A nice guy that was working his way up at the company he worked at. I didn't question things I made comments about. Like when I offered to double date with them and a guy I had been seeing. He refused, stating he wanted to be alone with Willow, and she didn't protest, just stood there. I should have seen it, her becoming different, less like herself the longer she was with him, to where he wouldn't even come into the apartment to pick her up but wait at the landing. She had said that it was to not miss reservations whenever he came. But I knew it was because he didn't want to see me. Then came the glares when I saw him, at me, at her. Like she said the wrong thing, or even just when she talked. Then came the bruises that she thought she hid well. I think they started after a company party, and Andrew thought she spoke out of turn."

"Apparently flirting with one of his coworkers. At least that's what she said when she came home in tears, when I saw the marks around her wrists, her neck. I wanted her to press charges because that was assault, but she fought me on it. I knew it would escalate. Because he was an abuser. I knew it. But also knew that he would push her away from me if Andrew knew I was talking about pressing charges. And I couldn't let that happen, so I tried to do things on my own regarding him. I tried pressing charges for her against Andrew. But I couldn't do anything because I wasn't the one that these things were happening to." Eric and Tommy listened to what she had to say, collapsing into Eric as he held her as she cried.

"Hey what Eric said is true, it's not your fault. You tried everything you thought you could without trying to get her hurt worse," Tommy said. She felt his towering presence next to her as she moved out of Eric's hold.

"Sorry, I rarely do that. Willow's my soft spot. I hate seeing her like that in that hospital bed. But I guess it's better than a coffin, right?" She questioned, trying to make a joke that she didn't even laugh at. As she wiped her face of the tears that had already managed to stream down her face as she explained Willow's past to Andrew to them.

"Again, dark humor. I know bad timing, considering every-thing. But before I become more of a blubbering mess, we need to go tell Micheal the update as he wanted us to when we saw him last time," Amanda said as she wiped at her eyes more and started walking toward Micheal's room—hearing Tommy and Eric's footsteps following her, them both to not press further on the matter because that would just make it worse.

Knocking on the door to the hospital room before entering, she walked into the nearly identical space to Willow's. Except there was a bigger window with a pleasant view. And a couch that was used for visitors to sleep on. Which was currently occupied by Evan lying on it, with a sheet over him; he was still wearing the hoodie and jeans from when she saw him running frantically to the truck, explaining everything that happened to them. The look of terror in that boy's eyes would never leave Amanda's mind.

"So, how is she?" Micheal asked as she smiled because of course, he would ask about her when he's basically in the same condition. And looked just as tired as she felt since waking up in the hospital.

"She's good, I think even better than you Swiss cheese" Amanda said as Micheal laughed, and winced at the pain.

"Hey, that was going to be my nickname for him," Eric said as he walked into the room, followed by Tommy as they both smiled at hearing Micheal laugh.

"Yeah, well, I think it's a fitting name for the both of them, don't you think?" Amanda asked, rhetorically.

Amanda's eyes landed on a woman looking frantically through the halls and looking at hospital rooms. The blonde hair stuck out to her as she watched her stop a nurse that was walking by that pointed in the direction of Micheal's room. And opened the door.

The woman's eyes landed on Tommy and Eric and walked up to the room, hugging them. And Amanda knew immediately that this was Pam, Micheal's ex-wife. Pam stepped past them, giving Amanda a quick scan from head to toe as her eyes narrowed at her questionably.

Pam didn't stop at Micheal's bed but went to where Evan was lying on the makeshift couch, waking him up, watching as the boy rolled over and saw his mom standing at his side.

"Come on, we're going home," she said simply, as Evan got up and looked at his dad, then towards Eric, Tommy, and Amanda with big eyes. But Evan didn't say a thing as Pam walked him out of the room and closed the door. Her expression changed immediately when she knew Evan was behind the door —crossing her arms over her chest.

"So, do you think it was a good idea for me to find out about this from a call from him?" Pam questioned, nodding her head in Eric's direction as Micheal narrowed his eyes at her.

"You realize I wasn't conscious, right? I couldn't exactly call you when I was on the ground bleeding out," Micheal said as Pam rolled her eyes, turning to Eric, Tommy and Amanda.

"I think we need privacy. Can you please leave?" She asked as Eric and Tommy went to move, and Amanda's hands shouted out to stop them. Pam's eyes narrowed at Amanda from that action of preventing the two men from leaving the hospital room.

"No, we aren't going anywhere. You aren't giving Micheal shit for this. It's not his fault. We made sure Evan saw nothing. You should be thankful he's not hurt like they are," Amanda said, feeling as her blood was boiling at this woman. Pam had the nerve to be mad at Micheal for not calling her when he was the one on the ground unconscious.

Amanda went to lunge at Pam. Pam rolled her eyes at that as Eric and Tommy went to hold her back, as Pam flinched at the move. "You have no right to roll your eyes. You didn't see how they were. Now I know why Willow doesn't like you, you're a bitch," she said as Pam looked at her with a sneer.

"You know I knew Willow was trashy, didn't know she came with trash bag accessories that believed everything she said. You realize none of this would've happened if she wasn't involved with him?" Pam questioned as Micheal moved on the bed, grabbing the remote and clicking a button as the nurse came over on the remote.

"Yes, Mr. Stanley? Do you need something?"

"I need someone removed from my room. Can you get security?" He asked as there was no answer as he put the remote down, and Amanda saw Pam's eyes go wide at that as she started for the door.

"Fine, I'll leave. I would rather do it on my own than be dragged out of here. Don't want to put any more stress on our son than what he's been through already tonight," Pam said, opening the door to his room and leaving, making sure that it slammed behind her. All Amanda could see before it closed was her pushing Evan in the elevator's direction.

"Well, I can say one thing with confidence. I know exactly why you filed for divorce," Amanda said, feeling Eric and Tommy's hold on her loose and leaving her as she turned to face Micheal.

"She was the one that filed for divorce, not me," He corrected as Amanda looked wide-eyed.

"Are you kidding? I mean, I can't see it at all. I can't believe she didn't even ask how you or Willow were doing," Amanda said as Micheal shrugged his shoulders or at least attempted to before wincing at the move. The door to the room opened back up. A man in all black came in.

"The nurse said you needed someone escorted out of your room?" He asked as his eyes scanned the room and landed on Eric, Tommy, and Amanda.

"No, that person left. It's all good here," Micheal said as the security guard looked at them.

"Alright, but I have to remind you that visiting hours are over. And you will have to leave the hospital," the man said to them as they nodded.

"Well, get some rest tonight. We came by tomorrow and visit you again," Eric said, coming up to pat Micheal on the hand.

"Yeah, we can even bring you stuff. Is there anything from your house that we can get for you?" Tommy asked.

"Only thing I can think of is my cell phone, other than that maybe a book or something because I know I'm going to tire of watching television quickly," Micheal said as they smiled at that, since he seemed to be a busybody, always doing something. So the hospital stay was going to be rough.

"Crap, I didn't ask Willow if she needed anything. Even though some things are coming to mind," Amanda mused as they started pushing her in the door's direction.

"Come on, you have tomorrow to figure that out. Let's leave before that guy comes back and makes us leave under his supervision," Tommy said as she rolled her eyes at that.

"Someone scared I take it?" She questioned as they laughed, opening the door and leaving Micheal in his hospital room.

Walking towards the elevators, Tommy clicked the button to go down as they waited. "Well, that went better than expected," Eric stated. Amanda knew what he was talking about, their interaction with Pam.

"Yeah, well, that's because I was there. I don't take any crap." Amanda stated as the elevator opened up, dinging as they got into it. Amanda felt as though a weight had been lifted from her. She knew that Willow and Micheal were in the right place and on the road to recovery.

THREE

The burning sensations racked over her body. *Willow struggled to cover the closest of the impact points that were close to her chest. Every breath she took felt like agony and was hard on her lungs.*

Sleep, just sleep. Rest. It will help with the pain if I just go to sleep. Willow thought, fighting the urge to keep her eyes open. seeing the night sky before her, smelling the chlorine of the pool she had landed in her nose, such an overwhelming scent. As she saw Micheal land near her, blood poured from him. Every beat of their hearts was making the blood flow out of them faster. Looking into Micheal's eyes, she saw the life in them dim as she struggled to move closer to him. Dragging her body or attempting to against the wet concrete. But with the loss of blood she couldn't drag her body any further than a foot.

She was hearing Carmen struggling in Andrew's hold, and the gurgling sound as he slashed her throat before he threw her over the side of the cliff.

Then the sound of the sirens, the cops coming to save them, and arresting Andrew. Or so she had hoped. Would they make it in time, though?

Willow woke up covered in sweat, looking around the room, and felt like it was real, the dream. She knew that what she experienced was false. Because she passed out before the cops or ambulances even came to help them. But seeing what her subconscious brewed up was something she was happy she never saw. Even if it wasn't true, it still left her startled and shaken. The look on Micheal's face, the light from his eyes and face slowly leaving him as he laid in a pool of his blood.

Willow went to get up, careful of her injuries, and took a hold of the IV stand like the nurse instructed before falling asleep. Her feet were going to the side of the bed and slowly down to touch the floor. The socks she wore that had the no-slip grip were helpful against the slick surface of the flooring in her hospital room—giving her traction to push off the side of the bed.

She walked a few steps around the bed and saw something out of the corner of her eye in the dark hospital room that made her jump against the bed. Willow didn't scream but inhaled a breath and froze until the person revealed themselves, moving out of the shadows.

Micheal took a few steps out of the darkness, hand on his IV stand with a handheld towards her.

"I'm sorry. I didn't mean to scare you. I was watching you sleep, and I didn't know if you wanted me to wake you or not. It didn't look very restful," Micheal commented as he took a couple of steps standing before Willow as she smacked him. And saw a smile grace his face at her action.

"I had a nightmare, mister, and I would have appreciated a

little help to wake up. Especially considering the company in the room with me. Which I might add is questionable Because I know you are in the same situation as me. How did you do it? Pay off someone?" Willow questioned with a raised a brow at him.

"You think I would pay a nurse to get out of my room? Because you are correct, I slipped my nurse some money to allow me to come here so I could see you. I got the full report from Amanda, Eric, and Tommy. And I just couldn't stay in my room after they left. My mind was racing. I came to see you, but you were asleep. My nurse had to make some rounds, so I promised I would stay put until she came back to pick me up for the walk back," Micheal admitted, and Willow could sense the {less than a man synonym/word}, radiating from him from that statement.

"I can't believe you bribed a nurse," Willow said, trying not to laugh, as Micheal's face too was sporting a smile at the thought as they both tried not to laugh.

"I can't laugh. Amanda made me laugh when she came to visit, and the pain was hell," Willow said, fanning her face and trying not to replay the image in her head of Micheal paying off a nurse and then being told he had to wait for her to come back to walk him back to his room, like a child.

"Hey, it's not that funny," Micheal said, trying to sound like he was scolding her but starting laughing. They both leaned into each other, laughing a bit, and then winced from the pain as Willow moved to lean back against the foot of her bed, taking a breath.

"That hurt, but it's your fault, being such an invalid and all," Willow commented as she turned to go to the bathroom.

"I'll just be a second. It's these IV bags. I feel like I've been up so much since Amanda left to go to the bathroom," Willow commented as she opened the door and closed it behind her. And she was out two minutes later, hands washed and was drying them on a paper towel, balling it up, and going to throw it in a nearby trash can. Willow closed the bathroom door and saw that Micheal was sitting in the chair next to her hospital bed.

"You ok?" she asked, squinting her eyes in the darkness, and saw him wince as he moved around in the chair to be more comfortable.

"Maybe paying off the nurse wasn't a good idea. She was giving me shit the entire walk over here," he said as he gripped the IV stand in one hand and the armrest in the other, wincing the entire time as he got to a standing position.

"Well, did you see me doing any fast movements when I was getting out of bed? You just got out of surgery. We both did," Willow reminded him as he sighed.

"Yeah, and then I got bitched out by Pam before Amanda went off on her. She was trying to say that I should've called her about Evan. As if I could be unconscious on the ground," Micheal said as Willow glimpsed a smile on his face.

"But seeing the look on her face when I paged to get security up here was pretty satisfying," he said, as Willow smiled.

"Oh really? I wish I would've been able to see that. How is Evan, though, in all this?" Willow asked. Remembering the look on Evan's face as she walked out of the pool and saw Andrew holding onto his shoulder.

"All things considered, he's fine physically. But I think we could all use some therapy after that fact," Micheal said as Willow nodded.

"You're telling me, I think I'm years overdue," she said as she went to sit gingerly down on the side of the bed to relieve the pain shooting up her legs from bearing her weight on her feet for so long.

"You know that is something that I never got an update on. I need to ask them where Andrew is. I would love to spit in his face, seeing him rot in prison for the rest of his life," Micheal said as the door to the hospital room opened and a nurse popped her head in.

"Come on, time to go," she said as Micheal rolled his eyes, as he leaned down to kiss Willow, before parting.

"See, even as a forty-year-old, I can't get away with being treated like a child," he said as Willow started laughing as the nurse's face practically screamed that she didn't think it was funny.

"You paid me some money to let you see your girlfriend for a few minutes. That doesn't mean that I'm just going to ignore my duties as your nurse. You just came out of major surgery. The both of you have. So, let's get you back into bed, so you don't end up spending months here trying to recover," the nurse said as Micheal started the slow walk to the hospital door.

Willow took that note herself and went to lie back in bed. Feeling the pain that had been traveling up even further to her back, leave her as soon as her back was on the bed.

"See you tomorrow. Maybe if my warden will let me see you,"

"Oh, if not, I'm sure our friends wouldn't mind playing messenger back and forth," Willow said, making Micheal laugh as he left her hospital room, closing the door behind him. She clicked the button on her control panel to turn the television on, flicking through channels, landing on a late-night show. And then click the button for the morphine, feeling the rest of her pain leave her after a few minutes. Before she found her eyes closing into a dreamless sleep.

FOUR

Waking up in the early hours the following day, Willow groaned, trying to turn her side from sleeping on her back the entire night, minding the IV in her left hand and moving slowly to lie on her left side, just for a second, knowing that if her nurse came in and saw her like this, she would get a talking to. About how that could affect her healing time.

After settling onto her left side, she opened her eyes, seeing that Micheal was occupying the chair converted into a bed. IV stand was next to him, and he was lying on his back in the chair with one of the flimsy hospital blankets over him. Her eyes scanned his face, seeing the bruises on his face that she didn't have time to notice the night before because of the dim lighting in her room. But with the morning light coming in, she could see the extent of his injuries, at least from the waist up. Her eye caught sight of his left arm, seeing gauze on his arm from a bullet taken out of him. Willow knew that feeling there were the same makeshift gauze bandages near her stomach and chest from the bullets, and some on her legs.

The door to her room opened up as her nurse, the one for the day shift. Her cartoon character scrubs stood out as she took ahold of Willow's chart, updating it, and smiled at her. With Willow waiting for her to go off about Micheal being in the room.

"You know he's the talk of the nurses' station. He's been on Gloria trying to revisit you after his night nurse let him visit you last night. I wouldn't stop pestering her since her shift checked up on you. They tried to negotiate by saying he would stop if you weren't doing well enough for visitors," she continued as Willow looked over at him, his chest slowly rising and falling in his sleep.

"Yeah, that sounds about right. I would do the same if I could get around like him," Willow said as she caught the nurse smiling at her.

"Yes, well, you got some in your legs, and the damage to your chest is more severe," she said, putting the chart back.

"Here's a menu for today. Pick out what you want for breakfast. It is going to be delivered soon. When you are through making your selection, just buzz me, and I'll come in and pick it up," Willow's nurse said before leaving with a wink as Willow wasn't really paying attention and looking at Micheal again.

Her eyes drifted back to the hospital menu and a sheet to fill out. Not just for breakfast. But also lunch and dinner for the rest of the day. Eyes scanning the menu, she heard a shuffling on her left. She slightly put the menu down and saw Micheal shifting in the seat, his brown eyes opening, moving his hair away from his face, yawning. A smile gracing his face when he noticed Willow was awake.

"Morning, anything good? I think my nurse shoved that at me like an hour ago, trying to distract me from getting over here. I ended up just selecting whatever seemed like it would be ok to eat," Micheal said as Willow smiled, as her eyes went back to the menu and the sheet they gave her to fill out.

"I think they hype up this menu too much. Amaretto French toast? I mean, I guess I could see it. I'm just happy I can eat and I'm not on a restricted diet after surgery. So that's a positive," she commented, not even hesitating at selecting coffee as one of the beverage choices.

"You think they would frown upon me just selecting coffee, or you think I would have to put something else as well? I mean, I am getting hydrated through the IV?" Willow questioned, and simply selected water as another option to avoid getting into anything with her nurse. Her eyes scan through the breakfast items, selecting a muffin to go along with her water and coffee. She knew why they asked for all the meals up front to be chosen for efficiency, of course, but felt like it was a chore to predict what she would want for lunch and dinner. So she just selected the safe option of a sandwich and water for lunch and pizza with a soda for dinner.

"Man, if I knew you would be so picky with food items," Micheal said, as Willow put her menu down and the slip of paper that was filled out with her options that she left on her table as she buzzed her nurse.

"What? That's a red flag for not dating you? I think it's a little late for that, both of us are full of holes everywhere." Micheal smirked at that as Willow narrowed her eyes at him.

"Don't you dare say anything," she said, as the nurse came in as Willow slid the menu and paper over to her, as the nurse looked in between Micheal and Willow, as Micheal was trying not to laugh.

"Did I interrupt something?" She asked as Willow rolled her eyes.

"Just him having his mind in the gutter, he's horrible," she said as the nurse smiled.

"His friends are worse, there's one outside at the nurse's station trying to pick up on a couple of nurses right now," she said, her voice full of humor, as she walked out. And Willow noticed Micheal's expression changed from humorous to sighing in frustration.

"I can only guess who she's talking about? Eric? Tommy? Hell, maybe even Amanda, I can see doing that. But I kind of got vibes from them that there are some sparks between them all so," Willow commented, trying to figure out who it was.

"Oh no, it's neither of them, Willow. I know who would try to hit on nurses while I'm in the hospital," Micheal said as the door to the hospital room opened up. A tall man wearing a suit with big hair walked into the room. He was placing his sunglasses in the front pocket of his suit—a smile on his face as soon as he locked eyes on Willow. Willow didn't miss Micheal's rolled eyes as he walked up to Micheal placing his hand on Micheal's shoulder, squeezing it.

"I had to come and see how my star was doing. Eric filled me in last night about it. I heard you got into a run-in with someone's crazy ex and that crazy groupie from years ago," he said, taking one of Micheal's in his, looking it over.

"Don't worry, didn't shoot off a hand if that's what you're worried about Vic," Micheal said as the hand on his shoulder was off immediately at that.

"That's good, but will you introduce me to this cute girl you're visiting? I went to your room and found it empty and your nurse filled me in on where you were," Vic said as he stepped up to Willow's bed, holding out his hand that was covered in rings.

"Vic, this is Willow, my girlfriend. Willow this is Vic Andersen, my agent," Micheal said as Willow took a hold of his hand and shook it lightly as Vic squeezed her hand in the shake, feeling the rings bite into her hand, as she let go of his hand at the added pressure.

"So your Willow? Glad to finally meet the new Muse of Micheal's work," Vic said as he looked from Willow to Micheal with a pleasing smile.

"Oh, I'm a new muse?" She questioned as she looked at Micheal with surprise, as she noticed that Micheal's face had a slight pink tint to it like it embarrassed him.

"What are you talking about? Since you've come around, he can't stop churning out the work. From what Eric has shown me, he will have a whole new collection to release soon for another tour of gallery shows. I'm even trying to get some international bookings as well," Vic said, proudly, as he clasped his hand again on Micheal's shoulder giving it a squeeze as Micheal winced.

"You realize I got shot at and went through surgery not that long ago?" Micheal questioned, as Vic's hand came off his shoulder quickly.

"Sorry, just proud of how hard you've been working lately. Which will be good, with no outlook on the recovery process," Vic said as he looked back at Willow, with a tilt to his head as he did so.

"You're the substitute teacher I keep on hearing about, not from Micheal, of course. He's quite quiet with nothing other than the business and painting and things, but from Eric, though. You're just not what I pictured at all. You're quite different from," Vic said, stopping as Willow frowned.

"You mean, different from Pam?" she said as Micheal rolled his eyes and went to pull Vic back around.

"You realize why I'm quiet about my personal life? Cause while you're a brilliant agent with getting me gigs for showings and things, and getting my work out there. You also were one person I confided in when the divorce was looming over my head and issues were happening in my marriage. And you used that private information to spout it out to the media for coverage. I certainly don't want you doing the same with this situation and with Willow," Micheal said as he looked up at Vic with contempt in his eyes.

"So please don't draw comparisons between Pam and her, especially when you never knew Pam. And you don't know Willow. Maybe we should continue this in my hospital room. Willow, if you're feeling up to it. Maybe I can come back later, 'cause I know Amanda and the boys are coming back and visiting," Micheal said as he slowly got up from his chair, kissing Willow on top of her head. Vic smiled at Willow, giving her a wide grin that gave her an unsettling feeling about the man—watching them both walk out of her hospital room.

FIVE

After the surprise visit from Vic Andersen, Willow got the vibe he was just a money-hungry person. Especially how he looked at Micheal's hands when walking into the room. She was just about to turn the television on since she didn't like the quiet when there was a knock on the hospital door, and then it opened. To a very familiar face that felt like ages since she had seen. Even if it had been only a couple of weeks.

"Julie? How did you—" Willow said as Julie walked in further carrying flowers and a basket full of an assortment of treats.

"Your friend Amanda called me off your phone. After what happened and how you left the school. I knew I had to call you to see how you were doing. And then I heard that this happened, and that this was your ex, the one from that day. So I just knew that I had to come by and see how you were doing," she said as she put the flowers and the basket on the tray. Willow opened the plastic from the basket and started looking at the items as Julie sat down in the chair.

"That's a little something from the staff they all pitched in after hearing what happened. All the teachers feel awful about it," Julie said as a frown replaced her bright smile.

"You mean about the accident? Or something else?" Willow questioned as she turned her attention to her friend.

"Well, there was, talk that we heard about. The district or the school administration thought about barring you from subbing at the school for making a 'scene'. Their words, not mine, of course. We all protested the idea. And it was right after it happened. A couple of days after that, the talks started. Maybe they will have second thoughts after learning what happened. But you know how it all is. Politics and how the district thinks the public will view them." Julie waved off.

"What do you mean? Like as if that was my fault? Are they blaming me for making a scene? Is it just that school or the entire district?" Willow replied as the beeping of her heart monitor started increasing. A worried expression crossed Julie's face at that.

"I'm so sorry, and I thought that your friend Amanda told you when I talked to her. I mean, I can understand why she wouldn't, of course. I'm so sorry to break the news to you like this. And no, I don't know if it's just the one school or the entire district," Julie explained, leaning back in the chair for a second before grabbing for the basket.

"How about we eat some of this expensive cheese and talk about other stuff? Like your new boyfriend?" Julie questioned. Changing the subject of the conversation as to not get Willow working up, taking some of the cheese and crackers out.

***

After Julie left, Willow was alone and full of emotions. She was anxious and saddened to know that there was talk of barring her from employment. After what happened to her at the school with her ex-boyfriend practically dragging her off the campus. However, Willow knew she had other options. Like going to get her master's degree like she always wanted, giving her more teaching opportunities. And she loves the academic side of it all, learning more about her subject. Or there was the route of getting a master's in education. Many teachers did to up their pay scale and gave them more experience to teach. Both options had their pros and cons.

She wished she had a piece of paper to write her list to help her decide. There wasn't a definitive answer, even if the district or school barred her from teaching. But she knew that to calm her anxiety, she would have to make a list of pros and cons to back herself up if she didn't have a job to go back to.

"Which also means no more health insurance either," she muttered, feeling her anxiety ramp up at the thought of that. The beeping of her heart monitor intensified, a nurse came in at the excessive beeping to check over her vitals.

"Are you ok? I heard the monitor and wanted to check on you?" She asked, putting her hand on Willow's shoulder.

"Oh, I'm fine. Work stress, you know?" She questioned rhetorically, feeling the nurse pat her shoulder.

"Well, that won't help with your recovery. But this might," the nurse said as she grabbed for Willow's chart and updated it.

"What would help exactly?" She questioned as the nurse looked up from the chart, all smiles.

"I've heard whispers that your boyfriend is getting discharged this afternoon. His recovery has been going well. Gave him instructions for aftercare at home. So that means he can come by tomorrow, not in the hospital gown to visit you," she said as Willow's heart rate went up a bit at that. And the nurse looked at her pointedly.

"Happy or stressed?"

"Oh, definitely happy. I'm glad he gets to leave here today. I just can't wait until I get to do the same," she said as the nurse nodded.

"You're telling me, as a nurse, it's nice when patients leave, that's the whole point. To get better and go on with your life. With how you are healing, it should be a couple more days, don't tell anyone I told you that. But the doctor is going to come by tomorrow to check on how you are. And from your charts and, well, that you are going to the bathroom on your own. I can see it only being a few more days, sweetie," the nurse said, springing hope into Willow at that admission.

"Oh, I won't be spreading that around. Thank you for telling me. That helps a lot to hear that," Willow said as the nurse left, making her feel better about her prognosis more than ever.

The sound of the hospital door opening woke Willow up from her sleep as she looked around the room and saw a set of feet coming into the room first before Micheal was wheeling himself into the room in a wheelchair. Her eyes looked him over, doing a double-take since she was getting used to the hospital gown and not Micheal wearing actual clothes.

"Hey, I'm getting discharged. Just wanted to stop by before heading down to the lobby," Micheal said as a younger male walked in, looking out of breath.

"Mr. Stanley, I'm supposed to be escorting you down to the lobby. You can't be going into random people's rooms," the young boy said as Willow smiled at that.

"It's fine, I know him," Willow said as the boy sighed, out of breath.

"Fine, just a couple minutes, cause I'm supposed to be getting another patient soon," he said as Micheal smiled, watching as the boy walked out of the room and someone else came in taking ahold of the wheelchair, Eric. And he had a smirk on his face.

"Time's up, you can talk to your girlfriend tomorrow when you visit her, now let's go before the kid notices that you aren't here," Eric said, taking ahold of the wheelchair and spinning Micheal around as Willow laughed at the look of shock that was on his face at how quickly Eric moved. Rolling him out of the room, and hearing shouts from the boy following them, along with protests from Micheal about not going down the stairs.

Willow is reading her magazine, trying to busy herself since she had nothing else to do while sitting in the hospital trying to heal. As she felt eyes staring at her. She looks up and sees Micheal looking up at her from his sketchbook with a smile on his face.

"What? What's with the smirk?"

"Oh, nothing, just realized that with you getting better, that means that the nurse will come in less frequently, which gave me an idea," he said as he goes to stand up from the chair, setting his sketchbook down on the chair, standing next to her hospital bed and looking at Willow pointedly.

"Come on, move over," he said as she looked at him. She did not believe what he was trying to get at.

"You want to share this bed with me? It barely fits me. And it's not made for two people," she said as he smiled.

"Well, you are quite on the smaller side, sure that will help. Now, move over, missy," he said as Willow laughed lightly, keeping in mind how laughing made her feel. She moved over to the side, as Micheal went to slip in on the side of her, his towering form looking comical, barely on the bed as he laid on his side next to her.

"I have a feeling you have an ulterior motive, and it's not happening. Remember our rule?" She questioned as Micheal smiled at her.

"I can convince you, like, for instance, by using the pout," he said, making his eyes look more prominent and sad looking, his mouth jutting down.

"Oh no, that will not work," she said as she saw movement in her peripheral vision and looked, seeing Eric and his blonde-ish hair making him noticeable as he stood at the end of the hospital bed, bag in hand that Micheal had brought with him.

"So, what are we doing exactly?" Eric asked, with intrigue on his face at the two of them in the hospital bed. Willow tried to push him out of the bed, but Micheal continued to smile at her attempts.

"Oh, nothing. Just trying to get Willow to cave and sleep with me, what's new with you?" He questioned, as Willow narrowed her eyes as Eric didn't bat an eye at that comical explanation.

"Well, I came to visit, but it looks like you're occupied with the free show for everyone to see. Hold on," he said as he grabbed one of the other chairs in the room and pulled it up. Placing his hands under his face, looking intently at Willow.

"God, I thought he was bad, there are two of you," she said, as Micheal finally got up from the bed, taking the bag that Eric handed him and then handed it off to Willow.

"Brought some clothes for you to change into, and other things to keep you occupied," Micheal said as Willow's hand went into the bag, feeling around. She was feeling the fabrics against her fingers and various papers, showing more magazines, stopping only at the feeling of a particular fabric, lace fabric. Her eyes were going wide at that.

"I'm assuming that Amanda maybe didn't pack this?" She questioned as she grabbed at a pair of lacy underwear, narrowing her eyes at Micheal.

"Or maybe she did, considering the last time. She packed me a bag to go over to your house. That included lingerie. But that certainly isn't the point. You get that I'm in a hospital. Comfort is key, not about you living out an odd fantasy," she continued, as Micheal chuckled at her frustration.

"It's a joke, granny panties are at the bottom of the bag," he said as Willow glared at him before throwing the underwear at him as he and Eric laughed.

"You're lucky if you see any panties, mister, at all. Ever." Willow warned placing the bag to the side on the table next to her.

"You could just go commando, it would solve the problem entirely," Micheal offered playfully back at her.

"You mean like you do? Not so little Micheal," she countered as Eric sat back in the chair shaking his head at this back and forth between the two of them.

"Is that supposed to be an insult? I think that's more of a compliment?" Micheal questioned back playfully, wiggling his eyebrows at her as she rolled her eyes, pulling the blanket off of herself. Gingerly making her way off the bed, walking to the IV stand in hand to the bathroom, mimicking the last statement that Micheal made in an annoying voice that had Micheal and Eric rolling laughing until the door was closed.

"God I want that," Eric said as Micheal went to sit back down, and look curiously back at his long-time friend.

"What do you mean? We were just joking around?"

"What I mean is I want to just banter away like that, knowing that someone else is in the room and not giving a crap. It was cute. I do like the two of you together. You fit," Eric said, leaning back in the chair, when a thought came to mind. His eyes went wide for a second as a smile graced his face.

"Hold on, one second. I have to get snacks. Don't you dare talk when I'm not here. It's like having live entertainment," Eric said as he got up from the chair and left the room

---

Eric was sitting in the chair, popcorn and other snacks in hand, watching television as Tommy and Amanda walked into the hospital room. Looking from Eric, eating, then to Micheal, sitting at his chair working in his sketchbook, and Willow reading a book.

"Sorry, it took a bit. The parking garage was hell," Tommy said as he leaned his back against the wall, and Amanda did the same since there weren't any more chairs.

"It's fine. You want popcorn?" Eric said, offering it up to both of them as they waved off the offer.

"You guys realize my nurse is probably going to bitch you all out for being here, right? We are definitely over the number of visitors at one time," Willow said as she looked at them, worried at the possibility of them getting yelled at by her nurse.

Just then, the nurse comes in, smiling at everyone as she takes a note of Willow's vital signs from the monitor and updates her chart without a word. Everyone remained silent until she left.

"I'm amazed she said nothing at all," Willow said, leaning more back into the bed, relieved.

"Well, a bribe helped convince her to look the other way," Eric said as Amanda rolled her eyes.

"Don't play like you gave her money. We saw the food you dropped off at the nurses' station that they were all eating," Amanda commented as Tommy laughed.

"Money, food, whatever it takes. Plus, they work hard. So they deserve something," Eric commented as Tommy smirked at that.

"Yeah, yeah, keep that thought in your head as a mask of what you were really doing. Like you did something good for once," Tommy said as he went to place his hand on Eric's head. With Eric dodging his hand and moving the bag of popcorn away from his friend.

"Trying to touch my hair. Yep, you just lost your popcorn privileges for sure now," Eric said, moving the bag over his head.

"As if I'm not taller than you and can get that bag from you in a second." Tommy said, rolling his eyes as he easily takes the bag from Eric's hold and starts eating some of the popcorn.

Eric stands up and moves his foot over Tommy's ankle as the young man falls to the ground. With Eric picking up the paper bag, looking down at the other man on the floor and rubbing his head where it hit the floor.

"Gosh, that must've been a long way to fall, oh giant one," Eric said, as everyone else besides Eric and Tommy started laughing at their antics.

"And you said we were the entertainment? I think you two are honestly," Willow admitted, trying her hardest not to laugh.

"Yeah, well, I could use you out of this hospital room. Let me tell you. I've had to spend time with these two, and I'm feeling outnumbered gender-wise," Amanda commented as Eric wiggles his eyebrows at that.

"Notice you didn't mention Micheal in all of that. But that could be because he just got out of the hospital. Regardless, Willow, does that mean it's an open relationship?" Eric pondered as Micheal narrowed his eyes at Eric's question, his hand connecting with the back of Eric's head.

"Jeez, it was just a question. You know any harder, and I could've sued for worker's compensation for trying to incapacitate me," Eric replied, rubbing the back of his head where Micheal tapped him.

SIX

A couple of days later, Willow was still in her hospital bed, and Micheal was in the chair as he had been every day since he had been discharged from the hospital. Only to leave when he had to pick up Evan from school to take care of him in the evenings. She would read the magazines, even the books that Amanda ended up dropping off from the apartment that her friend knew were her favorites to reread a million times over.

But every once in a while, she would stop reading and watch Micheal and how he worked when sketching. How quickly his mind worked as the pencil flicked across the page. He used one of his fingers to blend in harsh lines, leaving some of his fingers covered in the metallic gray coloring. He would keep it in mind about every once in a while, brushing his fingers against a spare paper towel to take off the graphite buildup on his fingers.

"You are staring again," Willow heard as she blinked, looking up at Micheal's face, but he wasn't looking at her at all but still working on his piece. The only sign that it had been him that said something for sure was the corners of his mouth were upturned, but in a way that he was trying to suppress the smile.

"Funny thought you were too busy working to notice anything," she countered, as she turned back to her magazine, only then realizing Willow had opened it to a page that she had not even bothered to read before.

"Well, when a pretty girl is watching me work, trust me, I notice," he commented.

"Uh-huh, to get us off this topic, well, what time were you discharged?" Willow questioned as Micheal looked up from his sketchbook, stopping his work.

"Oh, that wasn't until the afternoon. Don't expect the hospital staff to get to discharging you until then, Willow," he said as she groaned.

"I just want to get out of this hospital gown and take a damn shower. Wash my hair and just get into my clothes," Willow said, falling back dramatically against the hospital bed as Micheal laughed.

"Oh, I am sympathetic to your plight," he said as he turned back to his piece, shaking his head at her.

"Uh-huh, I doubt it," she said, sticking her tongue out at him as he looked at her with a raised brow.

"You want me to draw that expression on your face? It might just stay on your face if you hold that any longer," Micheal said, focusing back on his piece, not considering Willow rolling up the magazine in her hand and throwing it at his head as it hit him.

"If you want to do any damage, I would use something heavier," Micheal said, picking it up from the floor and placing it on the side table.

"I was hoping for paper cuts," she joked as she clicked the remote on. She was noticing out of the corner of her eye that Micheal had stopped drawing. He was taking time to open and close his right hand like he had been doing the other visits.

"You ok?"

"Yeah, my hand just gets stiff, that's all. Vic was talking about physical therapy in one breath and then more pieces. It's like either he wants me to heal properly or not," he said as he opened and closed his hand again. He put the notebook on the side table with the pencil and wiped his left hand that he had been using to blend in the lines.

"You think your nurse would come after me for washing my hands in your sink?" He questioned, showing his graphite-covered hands.

"Not unless she catches you. I have to say I'm going to miss her. She was a hard-ass, of course, but I kinda liked her," she said as Micheal walked to the bathroom and washed his hands vigorously with soap and water until they were clean of the pencil graphite.

"So basically, this is going to be the longest day ever just waiting until I'm discharged," Willow complained, as Micheal raised both eyebrows at that quickly and then went back to a neutral expression.

"What? I've been a good patient this entire time. We've both gone through hell," Willow said as Micheal sat down next to her, grabbing her hand and putting it in his.

"Yeah, I know, but think of it this way, it's your last day here. Then you can start adjusting back to normal life," Micheal said as Willow felt the anxiety come, remembering that she might not even have a job to go back to when she gets discharged from the hospital.

"Yeah, normal life," she said as she moved her hand out of his, trying to take a couple of deep breaths as Micheal tore one page from his sketchbook out. Then rifling through a bag that he brought his sketchbook in, pulling out another pencil.

"Remember when we tried working your frustrations out in my art studio? How about you try that now, get it out on the page? Hell, even if you aren't drawing, you can write it out?" He offered as Willow took the pencil from Micheal's outstretched hand. Their hands touched briefly, sending sparks up Willow's arm at the contact that made her smile—arranging the piece of paper against the magazine on her lap—bringing her knees up to use as a makeshift table. Since the angling with the one on wheels that she ate her meals from wouldn't be the right angle to write or draw on. Willow looked at the paper and wondered whether she wanted to write out her frustrations or draw them out.

She tapped the pencil's tip on the bottom of her chin in thought as she heard the vigorously scribbling next to her. Her eyes were going back to watching Micheal draw. His face was down, but she could see the slight furrow of his brow as he concentrated on the image that he was working on. His shoulder-length, dark, wavy hair was slightly moving to cover his eyes as he worked. He was taking moments to stop and blend certain parts again with his left hand.

"You're staring again," he commented lightly as Willow smiled.

"Hey, I just find watching you work more interesting than trying to get this frustration out of me and onto the page," Willow commented before looking down at the blank page and taking the pencil in her hand. She knew she was only a beginner but had some basic knowledge from an art class in high school. Even if that felt like that was a million years ago. It was something that was a skill set she knew she could grasp from as she looked back at Micheal with a smile, making a light sketch on her piece of paper.

After both she and the doctor completed the paperwork, he had determined that she was well enough to be discharged from the hospital. She was gathering her belongings and the things that Micheal had brought in each visit. Getting a knock on the open hospital door, they both turned expecting an intern coming with a wheelchair to take her down to the lobby. But it was Eric and Amanda.

"Thought I would pick up your friends so that we could see you off from here and back at the apartment," Eric said Willow shook her head, not at Eric but Amanda.

"You didn't have to come here. Micheal is giving me a ride back. And you're picking her up at the apartment?" Willow questioned, as Eric turned pink at the questioning as Willow looked from him to Amanda, who was too busy helping collect things to notice Willow staring at her.

"It's nothing, just more convenient, really," he said, nervously scratching the back of his neck.

"Oh, I have a copy of the new keys for the front and the apartment door," Amanda mentioned, putting them in the bag.

"So you persuaded the super to change the keys, I mean even the front entrance?" Willow questioned, not looking at Amanda but at Micheal, knowing that he would've done something like that.

"With the right amount of money, yeah," Eric said with a shrug of his shoulders, as Willow noticed that the pink tint on Eric's face had not gone away at all. Which she thought was from being embarrassed about being put on the spot, but there must be something else. Eric shared a look with Micheal as Willow narrowed her eyes at them.

"You're both acting weird. What's up?"

"We kinda found out some information," Eric said. He looked up at Micheal expectantly.

"I was checking my messages. They never found Andrew.

He ran from the scene. And Carmen, right? We both saw her get shot and thrown over the side of the cliff by Andrew, right? Yeah, her body wasn't recovered at all from the scene," Micheal said slowly.

"That's why I had to get those locks changed at your place. It wasn't safe. At first, I was going to have you stay with me, but," Micheal said as Eric patted his shoulder. Willow sat back down on the hospital bed, feeling her headache and her heart race.

"Andrew was not caught, and Carmen's body was never recovered. They are still out there somewhere, just waiting" she said more to herself in a low, shaky voice. Her fleeting happiness about being discharged was forgotten.

"Hey, I can have Larry with you at all times, it's fine," Micheal said, putting his hands on her shoulders and looking her in the eyes.

"You can't do that. He's hired to protect you. I have the gun. I can get another one and keep one in my car's glove compartment. One in my purse and another one in the apartment," she said slowly, trying to wrap her head around all this information, just as another knock was on the hospital door. With a hospital intern waiting with a wheelchair at the door. Willow's shoulders drooped at that as she got up and got into the wheelchair. With Eric, Amanda and Micheal all following behind her and down to the hospital lobby.

Willow got out of Micheal's suburban, new keys in hand as she walked up to her apartment with him following right behind her.

"Guess I'll have to get you a copy of these, maybe tomorrow," she said, yawning, opening the door to the entrance just as Eric's car pulled up with Amanda inside.

"You and I both know something is going on, right?" Willow questioned rhetorically as Micheal smiled.

"Oh totally, between the three of them, I suspect. But whatever makes Tommy, Eric, and Amanda happy, right?"

"Definitely," she said as she hugged him, not wanting to let go of him, as he pulled away, bending down to kiss her as she pulled away, yawning.

"Sorry, just really exhausted. I'll talk to you tomorrow," Willow said, opening the door as Amanda got out of the car and walked up to the pair.

"Come on, Willow, you need to take a proper shower. I know you don't know it, but there's an aura of stink just around you right now," Amanda said, gesturing to Willow's entire form as they both laughed. Micheal waited until the front door closed before getting into his car, leaving just as Eric did the same.

"Hey, I blanked and needed to go to the grocery store to get some things. You want to come with me?" Amanda asked. The door to Willow's room opened. She walked out, brushing her hair.

"Yeah, totally I want some good food after all that hospital food," Willow said, running the brush one last time through her red curly hair that was less than its usual curliness because of being slightly damp still. She walked into her bathroom to put the brush down and then grabbed her purse and walked out the door to the grocery store with Amanda.

"So are you going to continue denying something is up between the three of you, or are you going to confirm it?" Willow questioned as Amanda parked her car, turned off the engine, and looked at Willow with raised brows.

"Girl, I honestly do not know. Seriously. I mean, they're both cute, and well, we were going through it while you both were in the hospital. I still feel guilty that this is all kinda my fault if I hadn't—" she said as Willow stopped her, shaking her head.

"No, none of this is your fault. You just introduced me to Andrew, that is all. You aren't to blame for any of this," Willow said, putting her hands on Amanda's shoulders, squeezing them as she rubbed her arms affectionately.

"You're my best friend, and I love you, girl. Don't you dare blame yourself for any of this at all? Except maybe me filling up the cart with unnecessary items, though," Willow said as she got out of the car fast. Willow left Amanda fumbling with her seatbelt before getting out and running after her friend towards the grocery store entrance.

"God, Willow, I swear if you put just all junk food in the cart," Amanda said as Willow grabbed a cart and they went inside, starting at the produce section.

Amanda looked at the salads and their expiration dates as Willow handled the cart, gripping her hands on it. She was flexing her hands when she gripped it too tightly as someone came up behind her. Thinking she was blocking the section that the person wanted to look at, she moved forward.

"Sorry that I'm in your way," she said, with no response from the other person.She moved onto another section, and the same thing happened and she moved away from the person apologizing as she went.

And after the third time, she ended up turning down the aisle that connected to the produce section, which was the alcohol, feeling her heart race and her face and chest were hot. She took a couple of breaths and looked at the bottles of liquor, grabbing for the cinnamon whiskey gallon bottle instinctively. Willow heard a crash next to her, a stray bottle of liquor falling onto the ground. Causing her to freeze when putting the bottle in the cart. Her mind was going to the attack and the sound of gunshots ringing in her ears. She took hold of the cart, continuing down the aisle and turning, not paying any attention to where she was going, just feeling her heart rate speeding up in her chest and the fight or flight instinct kicking in.

SEVEN

"Willow? Willow?" Amanda said as she turned around in the produce section, not seeing her friend anywhere, with a bag of pre-made salad in her hands. Her eyes were scanning the produce section and not seeing Willow anywhere with the cart.

"I would've half expected her to be looking at the ice cream at this point like she usually does." Amanda thought aloud as she continued her search for her friend. She walked around the produce section and back to the last aisle where the alcohol was, thinking that her friend might be there. All she saw was one of the grocery store workers cleaning up a spill.

"Hey, did you see a girl with curly red hair in the produce section? She's my friend, and I can't seem to find her?"

"Yeah, someone broke this all the floors, and a girl was down here getting some whiskey, then booked it out of the aisle pretty fast. She looked pretty spooked," the man said as Amanda sighed.

"God, I knew it. I knew that taking her out here wasn't the best idea. But I thought she would be ok. She seemed ok out in the car." Amanda said, trying to control the panic that she was starting to feel at not spotting Willow at all. Amanda looked around, going down every aisle, looking for her friend's curly red mass of hair. Going down the ends of aisles and peering into them and not seeing her anywhere. Panic set in, and her mind raced.

"What if Andrew got her? Saw that she was alone and snatched her?" She said, shaking her head, trying to not dwell on that thought that could actually be a possibility. She went down the other aisles, checking the other side to see if she missed her from that side. And after walking back into the produce section, she walked back to the liquor area, wondering where the hell her best friend was. She had her hands on her knees, trying to catch her breath. She heard a noise. It was so slight that she stopped everything and listened, her head turning in the direction of the dairy case. The sound of someone crying behind the dairy case.

Amanda burst through the back doors next to the liquor section that was for the grocery store staff. Going through to where the team would stock the milk and seeing Willow huddled in a corner, shaking and crying on the floor.

"Hey" was the only thing that Amanda could even think of saying, going to her friend and seeing her red-rimmed eyes and her face covered in tears. Her face and chest were both red and blotchy from crying as Amanda sat down next to Willow. Draping her arm over Willow's shoulders and pulling her in closer to her, and sitting in silence for a minute.

"You know you had me so scared. I thought Andrew up and kidnapped you. What happened?" She asked.

"I don't know. One second I was getting whiskey. And then I heard a crash. It must've been someone breaking a bottle. And then I open my eyes, and I'm back here. I don't remember running back here at all," Willow admitted.

"Well, I'm glad it was here and not the parking lot. You

should've told me if you weren't ok. I would've understood if you wanted to stay at the apartment while I went shopping."

"Yeah, that's the thing. I thought I was fine too. Guess not," Willow said as she laid her head against Amanda's shoulder. Amanda shifted, getting onto her feet, as she held out her hand for Willow to take, getting her friend up on her feet.

"Come on, let's get the stuff in the cart. Get some junk food and go watch an awful movie," Amanda said as they walked out together from the stock area. With Amanda standing next to Willow the entire time as they picked up things for the week. With Amanda noticing her friend's shaking hands the whole time, handling the cart.

Getting back to the apartment, they quickly put all the groceries away. Amanda was grabbing some shot glasses and the gallon bottle of whiskey. Willow was giving her a skeptical look the entire time. Amanda walked to the couch and sat down, and set the shot glasses down along with the bottle. She was patting the spot on the couch next to her.

"Come sit down, and we can make it a drinking game,"

"I don't think that's such a good idea? Don't you have to work tomorrow?" Willow questioned as Amanda noticed a look on Willow's face at the mention of work.

"No, you just got out of the hospital. I called in sick for tomorrow, just for this reason," Amanda said, picking up the shot glasses and passing one to Willow.

"So you get any information when you got discharged? When can you get back to work? If you need physical therapy?" Amanda questioned absentmindedly, picking up the remote and searching the channels on TV to see if there was a movie that was already on that they could watch.

"I have a note. The thing is, is that I don't know if I have work to go back to," Willow said with a sigh as she took the cap off the bottle of whiskey and started pouring some into her shot glass and then grabbing for Amanda's and filling it.

"Um, what are you talking about? You don't know if you are subbing for the district?"Amanda saw Willow's look on her face at that comment. The anger was flashing in her friend's eyes at her.

"Yes, I knew about it. Julie told me, and I just didn't want to tell you right now. You have enough to deal with, and she said she didn't know the status of if it was just the one school or the district. Or even if it was going to be happening at all. Just that there was talk that she heard from the administration,"

The tension in Willow's shoulders left her as she took the shot, grimacing against the taste and then pouring another one quickly. Amanda gritted her teeth at the thought of having to keep up with Willow because she knew that when Willow drank out of being stressed or worried, that she would have to pick her friend up from the floor later and put her in bed.

"I just can't believe they are blaming me for this. As if it's my fault. I just want to get up in their faces and explain everything. As if I asked to be treated horribly by that man,"she said, taking another shot.

"Hey, slow down, if you don't, there's going to be cinnamon-scented vomit on the floor real quick," Amanda said as she slowly took her shot, tossing it back quickly, not really blaming her friend for wanting to find release in drinking especially with what she had been going through.

"Let's look at it this way. We will not think about it until there's a sure answer by the district. And take this time just to heal, you know? Since you just got discharged and everything. How long do you think the district would let you take off if you were working for them?"

"I don't know. I mean, I'm a sub, I'm the one making my hours. But if I were a teacher, maybe a day, a week if I were grieving a death," Willow said slowly, as she leaned back into the couch.

"Well, I say take a week as a grieving time for the old Willow," Amanda said as she set her shot glass down and sat back against the couch, too. She was putting her arm over Willow's shoulders and pulling her close to her.

"Yeah, grieve the old Willow. I like that," Amanda heard Willow say in a small voice as Amanda smiled.

"Hell yeah, 'cause Andrew doesn't know what he unleashed. Hell, you survived being shot by his ass. Now he's got hell to pay if he crosses paths with you or Micheal. Or anyone of us," Amanda said, rubbing her hand against Willow's shoulder.

"How about you go get some rest, I'll make breakfast in the morning, or we can go out? Have brunch with unlimited mimosas? Maybe invite the guys?" Amanda offered, as Willow smiled.

"Uh-huh, just me and you. Bullshit, you are so going to take the chance to invite Eric and Tommy. You have a thing for both of them," Willow said, smiling as Amanda felt her face heat at her friend's words about the two men, who she couldn't bring herself to even choose between. Despite the fact that she had gotten closer to the two of them since Micheal and Willow had been in the hospital. Amanda discovered that while both men were different and almost complete opposites in some aspects that they both brought out different sides of her. And she liked that.

"Yes, well, that's just under the assumption that they aren't busy," Amanda said, trying to get her thoughts off the two older men that seemed to encompass her thoughts suddenly.

"Oh, just say unlimited mimosas, and I'm sure they'll come running. Especially if you're there," Willow said with a smirk as she poured another shot for both of them. They were clinking the glasses together before taking the shot. Both were grimacing at the harsh cinnamon whiskey taste hitting the back of their throats.

"Ok, and with that, I'll be putting this away, or else we might actually finish the entire handle of this gallon jug and then get alcohol poisoning," Amanda said as she got up, grabbing the gallon container of whiskey and putting it in one cabinet in the kitchen. And the glass shot glasses in the sink, looking back and seeing Willow yawn and get up from the couch.

"You're right, going to go to bed anyway. Especially with the promise of some good food tomorrow," Willow said as she got up, hugging Amanda.

"Night, see you tomorrow morning,"

"Night," Amanda said, trying to clean the shot glasses and squeezing Willow in return, waiting for the click of her door to be heard. As she leaned against the counter, with the water running, she was feeling the tears start well up in her eyes, putting the shot glasses in the drain. Amanda was grabbing for the gallon container of the whiskey and walking into her room, setting the bottle on her nightstand as she went to change into pajamas. Which was an old t-shirt and pajama shorts that no longer had its matching shirt to go with it—crawling in bed and clicking on TV— she took off the cap off the bottle and took a swig of the whiskey, trying to focus on a whatever late-night show that was on the screen. But she couldn't help replaying the picture in her head of when she saw Willow in that back storage room, huddled in the corner—shaking and looking so small and so sad and scared.

She leaned over, grabbing for her phone on the nightstand, going through the contacts. Her finger hovering over a name in her contact list, thinking if she should even call at this late an hour. She shook her head as her finger clicked on the name and put her phone up to the side of her face, hearing ringing.

Waking up the following day, Amanda groaned against her pillow. Feeling as if a semi-truck came in and just rolled all its tires over her head. She opened her eyes, hurrying to cover the blinds and getting up from bed, seeing the gallon container of whiskey on her nightstand. Not completely gone. But the difference from what they drank before Willow went to bed noticeably was down. She also saw her phone and a vague memory of talking on the phone to someone, or even multiple people. She couldn't remember.

"Have to stop calling people when I'm drunk. Maybe get a Breathalyzer app installed that shuts the phone down if I'm drunk or something." She muttered to herself as she got up the whiskey container in hand, as she opened her bedroom door slowly and peeked out to see if Willow was up yet at all. Not seeing her red-headed friend in sight in the living room, she opened the door and walked into the kitchen, placing the bottle back where she had placed it before, closing the cabinet with a sigh.

At the sound of ringing, she jumped where she was standing, looking down at her phone as if it was the devil himself, as she glared down at it, clicking it—accepting the call with narrowed eyes.

"You know what time it is? I just woke up. And didn't want to be startled awake, that's what coffee and its bitterness is for,"

"You really think the coffee is the only thing that is bitter this morning?" The smooth voice of Micheal answered on the other end of the phone, chuckling at her.

"Oh, you do not know how bitter I can be, mister. So

what's up with the morning ring? Shouldn't you be dialing Willow and telling her all the sweet nothings that are just really pillow talk you should have after sex? Ah, wait, that hasn't happened yet? How are the blue balls working out for you?"

"Blue ball subject aside because I don't think I'm the only one having to deal with that. I'm sure that are two men you know well that could be in a similar situation," Micheal said, as Amanda's face heated at the topic changing to Eric and Tommy so early in the morning.

"But besides that, I just wanted to check in last night after your call you made to me. You ok?" He asked as Amanda gritted her teeth.

"Of course, I called you. Of course I did." she said wanted to smack herself for her stupid late night call to him as she heard him chuckle on the other end of the call as she continued.

"Peachy, I'm fine, just, you know, a drunk dial, but you know that reminds me. I mentioned to Willow last night about going to brunch. Are you down to come along? Bottomless mimosas?" She offered, trying to change the subject.

"Oh, you already invited me last night to that, but then said you also wanted to ride with Eric and Tommy. You were very persistent about that little detail. I'm on my way to pick up Willow. So I think you need to get her up and ready," Micheal said as Amanda could hear the sounds of traffic in the background as she clicked off the call. Throwing her cell phone down on the couch and glaring at it.

"You and I are not in a good place right now, phone. How could you let me drunk dial and invite those guys along and INSIST on driving with them," she said as she walked to Willow's room, knocking on the door and opening it slowly. She looked in her bed and saw that the bed was nicely made, and Willow wasn't in it as she was standing in front of her closet, fully ready to wear a t-shirt and jeans and looking through denim jackets to wear.

"You're up already?"

"Yeah, Micheal called me earlier and said he was picking me up. And the guys were coming to pick you up. He laughed about that. Are you just getting up?" Willow questioned as she turned to look at her friend, still dressed in pajamas.

"Yeah, long night. I couldn't sleep. But you know me, it only takes a second," Amanda said, turning away and speed-walking back to her room. Closing the door behind her, she leaned against it, feeling butterflies in her stomach.

"Why the hell does this feel like a weird double date? Because it does?" She questioned aloud, as she went to her dresser, pulling out black faded jeans that had the knees ripped on them and a gray t-shirt to wear—making quick work of taking off her pajamas and throwing those in the hamper and putting on the jeans and t-shirt, grabbing for her sneakers and putting them on her feet. Going into the bathroom to run a hairbrush through her long black hair. And looking at her reflection in the mirror, specifically at her dark brown eyes, hoping she didn't look like how she felt. Which was close to a warmed over corpse after the amount of booze she drank the previous night.

Opting for a pair of sunglasses as well, she put them on, grabbing her purse, checking to make sure her keys were in her bag that had the mace keychain attached to it. And walking out of her room where Willow was waiting, texting on her phone.

"Hey, he's here, let's go down, and we can wait until the guys show up so we can go to that restaurant," Willow said, texting a response as they were exiting the apartment, locking the door behind them, and walking down the stairs.

"Hey, I invited you, not them. Come on now, open the door," Amanda said as she started knocking on the window of the passenger side door. Willow looked at her with a pout. They heard a clicking noise as Willow locked her door and waved bye. Willow and Micheal laugh as he starts up the truck and drives off, leaving Amanda standing on the curb. Crossing her arms over her chest, she looked up and saw Eric and Tommy outside the car they drove up in. They were just staring at her as they both leaned against the car.

"You did? Because we are supposed to be going with them," Eric said as Tommy just smiled, hopping in the driver's seat, starting up the car. While Amanda went to hop in the backseat, as Eric got in the passenger seat. Tommy stepped on the accelerator to catch up to Micheal's Suburban. The entire atmosphere in the car felt awkward. Amanda didn't know what to say since they actually saw her trying to practically fight to get into Micheal's car to avoid riding with them.

"You know what you did back there was funny, acting like you didn't want to ride with us to the restaurant," Eric commented as he turned to look behind the seat and at her.

"Or was that even a joke at all, hmm?" He continued.

"I mean, I couldn't imagine a reason you wouldn't just love us so much and all?" Tommy added playfully as Amanda narrowed her eyes at him as he looked at her through the rear view mirror with a huge smile on his face at her.

"Oh, I could never even think of an idea of why I wouldn't want to ride with you at all," she said, smiling but feeling mixed emotions inside. Her thoughts immediately went to the last time that she saw them when she blamed herself for being the reason that Willow ended up in the hospital. She flipped on her sunglasses to hide her eyes as she looked out the window of the car, feeling the heat of the sun on her face.

"I know I'm probably going to want a Bloody Mary wherever we go," Amanda said casually, as she noticed both Eric and Tommy smile at that.

"Oh, we know. Micheal told us all about that call that you made last night to him. Surprised you didn't call one of us as well. He thought so as well, but what are you going to do," Eric commented as Amanda groaned, feeling the pain between her eyes seem to be worse as the time progressed traveling to the restaurant, and despite the sunglasses that she was wearing.- Tommy turned into a parking lot as Amanda looked out at the restaurant, groaning at the sight of the building. The Mexican restaurant she had recommended to go to a celebratory dinner a week ago, after Willow and Micheal's first date.

She got out of the car, pressing her sunglasses closer to her face, hoping that would somehow help with her raging hangover she was experiencing—watching Willow get out of the passenger seat, looking happy and giddy as she walked up to Amanda.

"Like our choice? Told Micheal about this place and how we always come here on Fridays," she said, walking up to Amanda all smiles.

"Yeah, well, I'm getting a Bloody Mary. I honestly don't understand how you can just be so peppy and awake right now. You also drank last night."

"Yeah, well, I didn't drink as much as you did," Willow said as Micheal walked up to the both of them, as Eric and Tommy did as well.

"I heard Bloody Mary, I'm down," Eric said with a wink at Amanda as she groaned.

"Don't you dare get me started," as she walked up to the entrance of the restaurant with the rest of the group following her inside.

EIGHT

Following Amanda into the dark restaurant, Micheal at her side and Eric and Tommy in front of her. Watching as Amanda talks to the hostess that grabs menus for everyone and walks them to a back booth.

Sliding into the booth Amanda in between Eric and Tommy, which made Willow smile at her friend. Amanda takes off her sunglasses, narrowed eyes directed at Willow. Because Amanda knows exactly what Willow was smiling about, as she felt Micheal nudge her on her right side.

Willow ignored it and instead pulled up the plastic-covered menu, glancing at it but already knew what she was going to order. True, she knew she didn't feel as bad as Amanda looked, but again she didn't drink an extensive amount of that bottle herself last night, only a couple of shots. Ok, maybe more than a couple.

She was feeling her face heat as the memory of the last time that she had shots. It had involved Micheal, and a serious make-out session that ended up with cuddling in bed together. She felt her face heat at the memory, trying to pull her thoughts to the menu more, concentrating on the different choices to get her mind out of the gutter. But saw Micheal smile as he looked at her before looking at his menu as well.

<hr>

Exiting out of the restaurant, Willow wrapped her arm around Micheal's waist to steady herself. The Bloody Marys with Amanda was probably not a good idea. Then also mixing that with margaritas and tequila shots as well.

"We'll drive her back, make sure she gets inside the apartment just fine," Eric said as he helped Amanda into the back of the car.

"Hey, can we get through a fast-food drive-thru? A burger sounds great right now," Willow heard from inside the car as the guys laughed.

"Sure, since you drank your weight in alcohol practically," she heard before the door closed and watched them drive off. Her eyebrows furrowed in thought about them with her.

"She'll be fine. Plus, I think if they ever had a mind to do anything, they wouldn't. She would hand their asses to them, I'm sure. But they aren't like that at all," Micheal said as they walked to where he parked the suburban.

"You mean they are like you then," she said as he opened the passenger side door for her to get in. Not responding, just smiling at her comment, and closing the door once she got in.

"You could say that, I guess. But I think of myself as a gentleman," Micheal said as Willow turned to look at him.

"Oh yes, a gentleman that I know is just counting down the dates. Three more mister,"

"Interesting, wouldn't that count as one. Which means two more really," Micheal said, clicking his seatbelt into place as Willow narrowed her eyes.

"That was so not a date. We were with Amanda and the guys."

"Thing is is that you never set the parameters of what makes up a date. We could technically count that as a date," Micheal said, smiling at her. She slumped in her seat, pouting, realizing that he was, in fact, right on that. They never really agreed to what would count as a date.

"Fine, two more to go, gentleman my foot," she said as he laughed, driving them toward his place.

Once at his house, he fumbled with his keys at the front door. Willow looked at him skeptically, since it seemed like he was stalling for time.

"What's up? After the little date comment, you kinda went all dark and silent while driving back," Willow said as Micheal turned and leaned his back against the front door playing with the keys.

"Amanda mentioned calling me last night, right?"

"Yeah, god, whatever she said don't take it seriously at all. She says some crazy stuff sometimes. Cause I swear to god—" Willow started as Micheal shook his head.

"No, she was stressed. Probably still is, too. She mentioned an incident at the grocery store last night. Told me she found you in the back stockroom behind the dairy case," Micheal said as Willow closed her eyes and tried to take a breath, hoping that this wasn't happening and that this was all a dream.

"Of course Amanda would have told you about her anxiety attack at the grocery store," Willow said, rubbing her temples from the impending headache that was coming on. She had wanted to tell him herself. And not have her friend be the one to tell him about that.

"So what? You want to be my therapist and talk about it? I mean, hell, I got you guys all to come to that restaurant so Amanda could get over her hangover. We drank. I feel better. It's done. Now can you please give me the keys and get off the door?" She questioned as she held her hand to him to take the keys.

"No, I don't want to go in until we talk. It seems like you have triggers. And I—"

"I know. I know you want to be my white knight and help me. Sometimes you can't, though. Sometimes you can whisk someone away from their problems when it involves things you can't control alright," Willow said, snatching the keys from Micheal's hand and pushing him away from the door and opening it. And just leaving him standing at the entrance, her mouth agape at what she saw. Which was the entire house in shambles. Everything that she had remembered was elsewhere in the living room. Couches, rugs in the living room moved to the sides of the room.

"I was trying to tell you about it before you came in. It's been like this since I came home. I've been trying to work on it on my own. Larry has offered to help but I really just wanted to work on this on my own," Micheal said, watching as Willow took more of the house in, walking over piles of things that were on the floor. Stopping when she got to the sliding glass door that led out to the backyard. And staring down at it, seeing where Carmen had smashed her hand through to open it.

Then beyond that, looking at the pool in the distance, seeing the remnants of the police tape tied off on the trees. And the bloodstains near the pool. The two big patches of it that stained the concrete. Bringing it all back to her, as she felt her heart race, stepping Back and feeling Micheal's front hit her back. And his hands went to her shoulders, which were shaking.

"I just wanted to go into the studio, maybe get some aggression out on a canvas or something. I have to tell you when I heard that bottle break in the grocery store last night, and I was brought back here, mentally, of course. I thought it was a gun going off. But seeing this," she said, feeling as if someone was sitting on her chest, making it hard to breathe. She saw darkness on the edges of her vision before she blacked out.

Willow opened her eyes feeling cold and wet, suddenly. She found herself in a pool submerged in water. Breaking the surface, she looked around and saw Micheal treading water next to her, worry written all over his face and in his deep brown eyes, as he moved his hair out of his face.

"What happened?" she asked, looking around and wondering how she went from standing to suddenly in the pool.

"You passed out. I didn't know what else to do to wake you up, so I threw you in the pool," Micheal said as Willow made it to the steps that were on the pool, moving up to sit on the edge. With Micheal getting up and out of the pool. And standing at his full height and putting his hand out for her to take.

"You mentioned something about going to my studio to get your aggression out?"

"Yeah, but that was before. Plus, now I'm all wet. I'm sure you wouldn't want me to go in like this," she said, looking down at herself, as Willow took Micheal's outstretched hand to help herself stand up.

"It's my studio, and I call the shots. You can come in like that, since I won't be changing either," Micheal said with a smile as they walked into the studio and he flipped on a light illuminating the repurposed guest house.

Her eyes scanned the studio and understood now what Micheal's manager said to her before. That she had become his muse. Paintings littered the sides of the guest house all in different sizes. They were different things from what she could gather but everything was in bright colors. Which was something she wasn't expecting from his current work after the attack.

"Vic wasn't lying when he said I was your muse," Willow said, looking at a particular one that seemed to be a portrait of her sleeping in bed. Which had to have been something he sketched when she had been sleeping in the hospital. There were more that she had thought looked familiar, ones that he probably sketched out when she was in the hospital. Some were of her. But some were depictions of the attack, the aftermath, etc.

"It's my way of dealing with it. Or at least what my therapist suggested. Which has been working, other than talking to her since the hospital discharged me," Micheal explained, as Willow turned to look up at him.

"I had the same reaction you did when you came into the house. I knew I would stay stationary if I didn't have someone to talk to about it. Just be in this after accident headspace and not move forward. I know you've only been discharged for a day, Willow. But I don't want you to be stuck. Making it, so Andrew wins. He shouldn't be holding space in our heads. When that happens, he wins," Micheal explained, grabbing for a blank canvas.

"I'm going to go get some towels. I'll be right back," Micheal said as he left Willow alone with the blank canvas and noticed Micheal laid out paints to use. Taking a brush in her right hand, she took a breath and dipped it in one color, slapping it onto the canvas.

There was complete silence surrounding her as she started working on the piece—practically jumping out of her skin when she felt one of Micheal's hands on her shoulder.

"Sorry, I didn't mean to scare you. I didn't realize you were in the zone. Here," he said, passing a towel for her to dry her hair with, along with a card.

"What's this?"

"One of my therapist's business cards. I've been seeing her for years, on and off. After the attack rounded, we both knew the doctors told us to seek someone to talk to. It made me realize I need to go back to her more regularly. And maybe you should come by and see her. She mentioned she had an opening for tomorrow? Not like I'm trying to pressure you, but—"

"No, you 're right. I should talk to someone. I mean, the painting helps but talking it out. It seems to help," Willow said, taking the card in her hand and looking at it.

"Just one thing, though. Will you go with me?"

The next day Willow was walking out of one of the meeting rooms. Her eyes searched the waiting room and immediately connected with Micheals as he sat in one of the chairs, with a sketchbook resting on his lap.

"Hey,"

"Hey how was it? Not too bad, I hope," he said as Willow walked up to him as he was standing up. She hugged him without a word as he stood still for a second, taken by surprise by the hug.

"Thank you for coming here with me, even if it was just waiting outside. I didn't know I needed this."

"I'm glad I could help, even if it was a suggestion, really," Micheal said as he wrapped his arms loosely around her, returning the hug before they parted at the sound of the receptionist clearing her throat.

"Miss, don't you want to schedule your next appointment?"

"Oh, yes, sorry," Willow said, walking up to the little desk to talk to the woman, schedule her next appointment, and receive a little appointment card with the date and time scribbled on it.

Willow and the therapist talked about a schedule of coming at the end of every week and coming to talk about anything that was on her mind. Since that was the first meeting, Willow just spouted everything out about her past and her feelings. There still were more meetings to come up with, a plan for how Willow could deal with things.

Willow mentioned the painting and said that it had helped. The therapist agreed that was a good coping mechanism to get her frustrations out and journaling. But she also shouldn't be stressing herself out so much about work that she should take time for herself.And that's what she was going to do.They both walked out of the therapist's office hand in hand, walking back to Micheal's car.

"So, she told me I should try to take time for myself. And that reminded me. We still have a couple of dates to go on. When exactly is the next one going to be?"

The smile on Micheal's face was the only answer she got on the subject as he got in. He was leaving the next date, a mystery to her.

NINE

Feeling the sports car stop and the blindfold go off from her eyes. She could smell the salt in the air and could hear the sound of waves crashing as the blindfold came off her eyes. Willow squinted at the sun and looked around at her surroundings. The beach, the sand, the cool weather. And the Santa Monica Pier, the Ferris wheel at the end of the Pier.

"This is your surprise? I thought I smelled the ocean," she admitted as she turned to face Micheal, who was all smiles as she took the surprise date location in.

"Yeah, I thought we could walk around the pier, talk, and ride some rides. And eat some not so good food. What do you think?" He asked as Willow looked out at the pier that seemed to be full of people. The feeling of anxiety starting up in her head. The buzzing in her head and the overthinking about the possibilities of the date, what could happen, and how she would respond to the crowd size. Her hand immediately went to her purse where she knew she had some aspirin in her bag and an over the counter anxiety oil that the therapist had recommended to her in case Willow started to feel anxious. The feeling of

Micheal taking hold of her hand in his, his thumb moving to caress the outside of her hand, stopping the encroaching thoughts. With her looking back at him again.

"I know what the therapist said, that we need to have some fun and not think about anything. Just take it slow. And that's what we are going to do, okay? We won't do anything that you don't want to. But I can tell from the look on your face that you're already overthinking things," he said with a whisper of a smile on his face at his admission.

"Well, since learning that they couldn't find Carmen's body and they didn't arrest Andrew, and he's just gone. I'm sure you can imagine what my mind was going to," she said as Micheal smiled.

"Well, they tried once, and it didn't work, and that was in private. I hardly think they would try anything in such a public place. Let's have some fun," he said as he squeezed her hand before getting out of the sports car. Willow slowly followed as they walked to get a ticket for their parking spot to put on the car before walking up the stairs to the pier.

They walked hand in hand on the pier. Willow felt the buzzing in her head lessen as they continued to walk. Knowing they were in such a public place and Micheal's hand squeezing hers every once in a while helped.

"So, what do you want to do first? There are rides and games. We can do some of that first, then we can get food?" Micheal questioned as Willow smiled.

"Definitely want to ride certain rides before we get food," Willow said as he turned them in the direction of the ticket booth for the rides and games. He was placing the plastic band that was handed to him on Willow's left wrist, feeling the calluses on his hands on her wrist as she looked up at him, smiling at the look of concentration that was on his face, eyebrows furrowed as he tried to snap the two parts on her wrist.

"For someone that does painting for a living, you would think fine motor skills would be a thing?" She questioned playfully as he chuckled at that as the sound of the band snapping into place on her wrist was heard, and he smiled.

"Fine motor skills, you say?" He questioned back rhetorically as she snapped his band on his wrist in a second, as he narrowed his eyes at her speed.

"Guess me having smaller fingers helps, huh?" She said with a smile up at him, her hands leaving his wrist as he grasped her hand in his again. Walking away from the ticket booth and towards the rides.

"I say we do that one first pre-food eating, cause I know if I do that after eating I'm going to get sick," Willow commented, pointing out a spinning capsule ride.

"So you get motion sickness? Interesting choice considering,"

"Oh, I like those rides but in spurts," she said as she went ahead of him, practically pulling him along with her to go through the line barriers. Putting their wrists out of the ticket attendant to scan the barcodes on the bands. With Willow pulling Micheal to one capsule and sitting down with him. Waiting for the attendant to come by and push the restraint on, as the rock music that was playing blared overhead. The metal bar was pulled up and clicked into place, and within another minute, the entire ride started up. With Willow laughing and screaming as the capsule would spin them around the platform. As Micheal wrapped his arm around her as they shifted from side to side, spinning about.

"God, I'm glad I picked that first. It was fun huh?" Willow asked, as she walked off the platform and out of the exit with

Micheal slowly following behind on wobbly legs. When she didn't get a response, she looked back and saw that he was sitting on a bench just outside the exit and looked green in the face.

"Are you okay? You want me to get you some water?" Willow asked as she went to sit down next to him as he leaned back against the bench, head back, eyes closed, his shoulder length black hair moving away from his face.

"I think I just need a minute," he said slowly, as Willow shook her head at his reaction to the ride.

"You think that would be me, but I'm totally fine. Jostled. You sure you don't want some water?" She questioned, hoping that this date wouldn't end as quickly as it had begun.

"No, no, just stay here for a second. It'll only be a second. Thank god we are at the beach. The cool breeze is actually helping right now," he commented as Willow sat next to him. She adjusted her crossbody purse over to her right side, so she could sit closer to Micheal. Placing her arm over his shoulders and then moving down to rub his back affectionately.

"Are you sure you're fine? I'm more than ok with just sitting here and talking to you. Screw going on the rides," Willow said as Micheal, with his head still tilted up, opened his eyes at that and looked down at her.

"Yeah, but that was the whole point of this date. To go on rides and eat food and hang out,"

"Ok, well, I'm fine with just sitting here for a bit. Maybe that's the problem though, no food in your stomach," Willow said as she leaned against the bench, moving her curly red hair into a ponytail with a hair tie.

"Maybe. How about we just walk around for a bit? That could help," Micheal suggested as he got up from the bench, holding his hand out for Willow to take.

"Sure, we can go to the end of the pier. You said that breeze was helping," Willow commented as they started walking past the rides and games and further along the pier. We were passing people that had their fishing poles out.

"This was a good idea, though. And it's so nice out. Guess the therapist was right. We need time to not think about stuff," Willow said as she let go of Micheal's hand and stopped at the end of the pier, looking out at the endless ocean beyond them. She was closing her eyes and breathing in the sea's scent that seemed to take all of her overthinking away. Just wanting to enjoy this day and the moment with the person who she cared deeply for was sitting next to her. She opened her eyes and looked over at him. And he wasn't looking green anymore. And he was staring at her with a smile on his face, his dark eyes only on her.

"So I take it you're feeling better? Can I start with the old man jokes? Of not being able to handle one ride?" Willow questioned playfully as Micheal chuckled at that.

"One, I'm not that old. Just 'cause I'm older than you doesn't make me old. And two, it's funny considering you were the one that felt like they had to make a point of mentioning spinning rides and motion sickness for you to be commenting about my issue, missy. Just be aware this won't just go away," he commented as he took his hands off the railing, wiggling his dark eyebrows at her, and started sauntering off in the other direction. Leaving Willow standing confused for a second and blinking.

"Oh, we are making threats now? Interesting. I wonder what you'll come up with in return?" She pondered playfully as she went to catch up with him, feeling his arm go around her waist, feeling his fingers rub into her side as they continued walking around the pier.

Willow leaned her folded arms against the pier railing, looking out into the ocean and smelling the fresh air. In her peripheral vision, she saw Micheal do the same, and he wasn't looking as green as before and had something in his hands. A sketchbook and a pencil.

"You always seem to have that just up your sleeve all the time. Where were you keeping that?"

"Back pocket. You never know when inspiration will strike," he said, taking a deep breath, noticing how he would glance at the page and then back out at the ocean, and onto the shoreline —making quick flicking motions on the page.

"I was wondering if you were interested, that is. Would you teach me how to draw?" She asked, feeling the heat coming up from her question about asking him to teach her how to draw despite the cool breeze blowing on her face.

The answering smile and him moving to the side to pull her in front of him on the railing were enough as he propped the little sketchbook in front of them. And he was turning the page to a new one, clear of any marks. He handed her the pencil, putting it into her dominant right hand as his hand went over hers, applying light pressure as he used his hand to push hers across the page.

"You first start out with the horizon line. We'll draw the shoreline of the beach, but we need to do the horizon line first from our perspective, which would be about here," he said, pointing out where Willow was supposed to be looking. But all she could concentrate on was the feel of his calloused hand over hers as he pushed her hand into drawing the horizon line.

"Ok, and then what? Just draw what I see?"

"Pretty much. We are drawing on the shoreline. What works is having your eyes scan and moving your hand as if the two are connected," he said as Willow looked out where it looked like the shoreline ended, her eyes working their way back towards where they were slowly. Her hand glided across the page, making slight curves where the water met the sand. Feeling his hand slowly ease off. And his warm breath against her ear as he watched her progress from over her shoulder.

"That's good you're doing great," he said encouragingly, just as Willow's hand jerked to the side, creating a streak of graphite against the page. She pitched her head forward, groaning in frustration.

"You know it's all your fault, mister 'no boundaries and I smell good,'" she said, hearing and feeling him chuckle against her warmly.

"Well, what if I want to stand close to a pretty girl once in a while? Plus, you were leaning into me as well, little tease," he said as Willow felt his warm breath against her ear again and a whisper of something else before it was gone too quickly. Was it his teeth against her ear? He moved away slightly, taking the notebook in his hand and slipping it in his back pocket as she turned to face him. And he had a smug smile slapped onto his handsome face. The nerve of the man. Willow narrowed her eyes up at him as he held out his arm for her to take. She did as he pulled her quickly into his side.

"Just remember two can play at this game of cat-and-mouse sweetheart," he whispered into her ear, as she felt her face heat at the not so pure thoughts that were rolling around in her head at what he was hinting at.

TEN

After the minor incident with Micheal after the drawing lesson, Willow couldn't stop thinking about the potential of what was to come after this date. It was the third date, after all. Hand in hand, they walked along the pier. Willow looked down at the wristband.

"It's getting hot out. You want to go on that log ride?"

"Yeah, why not," he said as you both turned towards the line for the water ride.

"I always underestimate those rides," Willow said, flicking water off of her. And then running her hand through her damp hair, wondering exactly what it looks like since it's usually so curly.

Both Willow and Micheal walked off to the side, as Willow leaned against the railing looking up at the sun, hoping that being in the direct sunlight would dry the shirt that she was wearing. So it wasn't sticking to her like it was now.She could feel Micheal's eyes on her as he stood next to her.

"I have a little idea," he said as he grabbed her hand, pulling her in the opposite direction of the pier.

"But I wanted to go on more rides, and the food. I mean, come on, can't you let a girl eat some carbs?" She questioned dramatically in an exaggerated tone, making Micheal laugh and turn to face her.

His hair was damp from the ride as well. The dark t-shirt he was wearing was wet as well, making it stick to him more. Willow found her eyes scanning him up and down as he pulled her along behind him, through the crowd of people, and off the pier.

"So, where are you taking me?"

"You'll see," was the only answer that Willow got as he turned towards the beach and then rounded another corner. One second they were walking innocently along the pier and then on the beach, and the next second, Micheal's lips were on Willow's as her back was against one of the pier support beams.

His tongue slipped into her mouth, gently at first, which quickly became demanding. It's like nothing Willow ever experienced. Not with previous boyfriends. And certainly not with Andrew at all. She now understood why people describe kissing as melting because she felt like she was on fire, every inch of her, despite the cool breeze from the ocean feet away. Her fingers grip the back of his head, that was already close to her. But she wanted him even closer. He pushes her back just a little more against the beam, as the sounds of children playing on the beach are near the two of them. The thought of some children or even parents finding them was in the back of Willow's head.

She didn't care that much about it since his lips were on hers at the moment, giving her a good enough distraction from her inner thoughts. His face has the slightest amount of stubble that rubs against her face, but she doesn't care. Because he feels wonderful, his hands are everywhere. Willow tries to maneuver to get him closer to her. As he steps closer, taking her leg in his hand and wrapping it around his hips to bring him closer. She was feeling his body heat radiating off of him and onto her.

She moved away to take a breath. Micheal took the hint as his lips landed on her neck instead, still just as persistent licking and nipping at her neck. As she moaned when he got closer to her ear, he chuckled. He was rolling his hips into her, contacting her core with his obvious erection, helped by the wet denim he was wearing.

"God, you do not know how much I want you, Willow," he whispered in her ear softly before he nipped at her earlobe, as she pushed him away, as she took her leg from around his form and set it back on the ground.

"We can't be dry humping in public," she whispered.

"Well, see, my intentions were purely innocent. Just wanted to make out with you. You were the one that pulled my hair. After that, all bets were off on the 'innocent' part," he said as he did air quotes before moving back and trying to get his shirt to unstuck from him, making the definition in his chest standout more. He took a breath afterward, when he realized it would not stop until it dried. And leaned his forehead against Willow's.

"You don't know how much I want you though, truly, Willow," he said as she opened her eyes and saw that there was nothing, just love, not lust in his eyes. But love. And this was only the third date.But they did almost die together which would ramp up the process. When you've been practically through hell together, even if you know each other for a short amount of time, that would change the dynamic quicker. She took a hold of his hand, smiling up at him.

"Come on, lover boy, let's go get something to eat and then go on another ride. Maybe we'll dry faster," she said as she pulled him from underneath the pier, reemerging into the heat of the sun.

Hours later, sitting at a bench, most of the crowd was dispersing as the sun was starting to set. Being out in the nice mild weather made quick work of their clothes drying earlier. Which made it less of a distraction for Willow to be around Micheal.

"Hey, there's frozen lemonade. You want to share one?" Micheal asks as Willow follows his sightline and sees the frozen lemonade cart off to the side.

"Yeah, sure, why not?"

They both got up and walked over as he ordered it and started sipping at it within seconds of grabbing the plastic cup.Not a couple of minutes later, walking down the pier. Willow didn't know if it was the long day or walking around or the heat or just the sugar in the drink, but Willow could tell Micheal was off.

"Willow, Willow, what the hell is in this drink?" He says slowly as he grabs her closer to his side as they continue walking.

"Water, ice, lemonade, and mass amounts of sugar," she states simply, taking another sip of the drink and noticing it looked like Micheal was trying to look through the plastic cup.

"Are you sure? Like they could've put something in it. You never know. Because well Willow. I don't want to freak you out. But right now I can't feel my face," he said in all seriousness as Willow almost choked on the drink, laughing at his response.

"You can't feel your face?" Not sure if she was hearing correctly or not, she continued walking and felt as if she was pulling Micheal behind her.

"Willow, you're walking too fast. Slow down!" He complained as Willow imagined if Evan was this way when he was younger.

"Oh, it's probably true. Evan probably was like this" she muttered to herself, knowing that Micheal wouldn't hear what she said as he stumbled along while walking next to her. As she moved him away at arm's length, now questioning the lemonade that he drank and she grabbed for the cup and took a sip. And just as she thought it was just plain lemonade.

"Micheal, all you had was sugar. What the hell? People are going to think you 're drunk or something," continuing towards where the parking lot was.

One second, Micheal was fine, walking behind Willow slightly until he wasn't and he was running for the trash cans looking green and kinda pale in the face.

"Micheal are you ok?" Seeing him make a beeline to a section of the pier that had trash cans and bathrooms. And started heaving into one trashcan as Willow picked up the pace and held back his hair and rubbed his back.

Pulling himself away from the trash cans with his wobbling legs, he walked over to the bathroom to wash his hands and rinse out his mouth.

Watching him come outside a few minutes later, he looked more like himself. But also looked kind of ashamed as well.

"I think that frozen lemonade was a bad idea," he concluded as Willow passed a water bottle to him she paid for while he was in the bathroom.

"Yeah, I agree. And now we know. The combination of spinning rides, making out, junk food and sugary drinks doesn't compute with your system, *old man,*" she said as Micheal rolled his eyes but didn't really say anything else as they continued walking towards the parking lot.

"I think it's time we go home. I need Pepto and sleep," he said as Willow looked up at him and he looked tired.

"Sorry that I had to ruin our date," he said as Willow shook her head, slightly pushing against his shoulder laughing at him.

"Are you kidding me? It was great! Minus the throwing up and the dizziness and everything. But everything else was great. Best date yet." She said with a smile, as he smiled back.

"Just wait for the other plans that I have later on," he said as they got to the car and he unlocked the car door, as the wheels in Willow's head spun.

"You are just full of surprises aren't you?"

Opting to go back with Micheal to his house, Willow was happy to have some spare clothes from before the place's attack. She changed out of the dark gray t-shirt and jeans she wore for the day and into a comfortable pajama set, comprising a tank top and sleep shorts.She shook her head, remembering when she wore a matching pajama set at her apartment when he came to help her get over her nightmares.

"I think he would be my nightmare chase away cure. That and his mouth, of course." she said to her reflection in the mirror. Shaking herself out of her thoughts, she threw her hair up into a ponytail to get all of her hair away from her neck. And walked into the master bedroom, just as Micheal was grabbing for a change of clothes from his dresser. She went to lie down on the bed and turned on the television.

"Where are you going?"

"Taking a shower, a cold one thanks to you, firecracker," he said with a wink as he went to close the door to the bathroom. Willow felt her face heat at his very candid admission to what he was probably going to be doing in the shower. But she couldn't blame him on that account. Ever since they got in the car, she kept running the make-out session under the pier in her mind on repeat.

Her eyes looked at the bathroom door and saw that it had, in fact, not been closed all the way and was open just a crack. Curiosity getting the better of her, Willow slides off the bed, making sure that the television was up a couple clicks before opening the door slowly.

The water was running, and the shower door was closed. The hazy design of the door obscured her view a bit, but she could make out his form facing away from the stream of water. She could hear the slight sound of the slap of skin on skin, seeing his hand between his legs and cupping his balls with soap-covered fingers. He tossed his head back, bracing his weight with his other hand against the shower wall, groaning. His motions are fast as he quickly pumps his hand up and down with a loose wrist. He was then gripping tighter, dragging his hand down in slower, tighter squeezes. His chest was rising and plunging as he stopped. He was waiting a second before picking up pace again.

Willow watches her back against the open bathroom door. Watching him fist his hand around his long cock, repeating the loop of fast needy jerks over his hard length before slowing down again. He whispers her name as he switches from the quick motions and then to the slow ones.It hits her as she realizes that he's edging himself. Every time he jerks his hand quickly, his hips thrust to meet his strokes.

"Willow, Willow, please," escapes his lips in a whispered beg before groaning as he spills into his fist. And hearing him sigh and turn back into the direction of the spray of the shower to wash himself clean.

Willow, with her back against the door, could barely get her brain to function with the throbbing in her core at what she just witnessed. But it was a second delay before she fell back into the door, making a noise. That Willow definitely knew that Micheal heard. Not taking a second to even glance at the shower, she turned and closed the door behind her, running back into the bed and throwing the covers over her, and feeling the heat covering her face at her embarrassment. Sighing in relief that it was dark in the room, which would help hide the evidence that she just watched him jerk himself off in the shower while he imagined it was her.

The sound of the bathroom door opening and the light from within flicking off. And the smell of soap and aftershave hit her nose as she felt the bed dip to his added weight. Feeling the covers move and feeling him wrap his arm around her waist.

"Good night, Willow," he said as he felt his lips against her neck.

"I hope next time you can join me. I could've used a hand or two in there," he said before sighing contently against her.

ELEVEN

Willow tossed and turned in bed, images from earlier replaying in her head of Micheal in the shower. His head tipped back in pleasure. Turning on her back and looking up at the ceiling, she tried to think about something else and not the man sleeping next to her in bed.

"Why the hell did I have to walk into that damn bathroom? Even if I knew what he was playing at?" she mumbled to herself as she turned to plant her head under her pillow. Feeling the bed shift next to her, Willow moved the pillow from over her face and saw Micheal was lying on his side, awake and looking at her.

"You ok?" He said, trailing his hand up and down her arm.

"Just having trouble sleeping," she said dismissively, feeling him shift closer to her.

"I hope it's not because of nightmares," he said with all seriousness in his voice. Reminding Willow of the last time he visited her apartment, which was the first night in a long time, that she actually had a good night's sleep.

"No, no, it's not," Willow says, taking a hold of his hand in hers, stopping the motions that he was making along her arm. He was leaving goosebumps all over her body in his wake, which oddly combined sensations. Willow was hot all over from the thoughts that had been replaying in her mind about Micheal in the shower and then the goosebumps. He took his hand out of hers, caressing the side of her face. And she knew he could feel the heat on her face.

"The air conditioning is on, so that's not the cause. You must be turned on," feeling Micheal's fingers trailing up her arm again.

"Thinking about how you were watching me in the shower? You know I've been doing that since we started this whole dating thing, since the dating rule and everything. I couldn't stop thinking about you at all," he said as Willow was trying to control her breathing.

"But I'm more than willing to wait whenever you are ready," he said, going to move away from her, but she stopped him, looking over at him in the darkness.

"That's fine, but you've got me all worked up over here to where I can't sleep." Pulling him closer to her, to where she was only inches away from him.

"So, what are you going to do about it? Since you are the one that is getting me all hot and bothered?" Willow asks. Micheal trails his hand up and down her arm again, as Willow could see more of him as her eyes adjusted to the darkness. Feeling his thumb caress against her hardened nipple.

"You and your cute little tank tops," he said, making her think his mind was on the apartment and when they were interrupted by Amanda coming into the apartment after her shift was over. One second he was next to her, and the next, he was looming over her, his weight more towards his upper arms and his lower body. His hands were on her breasts, both thumbs rubbing circles over her hardened peaks.

"Wow, I should've given you the go-ahead a lot earlier if you were going to be so enthusiastic about it."

"Enthusiastic is an understatement," he said as he moved the tank top up, revealing her breasts as his lips went to cover one of her nipples, circling his tongue around one. He was kneading her other breast in his hand. Leaving Willow a moaning mess, throwing her head back into the pillows, eyes closed. Then his hands were gone from her breasts, moving lower and stopping at the waistband of her pajama shorts.

"I have an idea on how to get you off, both of us, off that it's going to require these to come off," he said as his fingers slid under the waistband and pulled them off of her but then stopped.

"Unless you don't want to," he said as Willow opened her eyes and looked up at where he was now kneeling in between her outstretched legs, just waiting for a response. With his hands at his sides.

"No, I want to," she said as he nodded just once as his hands went back to her waistband, pulling it down along with her underwear, leaving her bare. He leaned his weight onto his ankles as he removed his t-shirt and then got up from the bed, taking off the pajama bottoms he had been wearing. And once those came off, his hard erection sprang forward. He kneeled back onto the bed in between her legs. Willow's eyes were on him as he fisted his cock in his hand, his dark eyes looking at her face and nowhere else. A smirk on his face the entire time.

"Let's get each other out of this predicament, get you some relief," he said closer to Willow, his left hand going to her nether regions. Using his left hand to spread her open, running his thumb over her clit slowly. While running a finger up and down, collecting her wetness to apply on her clit.

"God, you're so wet already," he said as he leaned forward

and ran his cock against her, stopping just as it touched her clit. Causing her to jolt where she was laying down.

He rocked against her in a steady rhythm. He started groaning, which made the heat pool in her lower belly, as she started to also move against him as well. In a counter rhythm, to match him as they were grinding against each other.

"God, you don't know how long I've wanted to do this, to touch you like this," he groaned, taking one of her nipples and pinching them in between his fingers. Sending another set of jolts, making her move quicker against him.

"Yes, it feels so good," she moaned in response, feeling him quicken his pace, making a point of rubbing his cockhead against her clit every time, feeling herself getting closer and closer over the edge.

"Come on, sweetheart, come for me. I want to be covered in your cum, babe," he said as his thumb went to glide over Willow's clit. The combination of his words and his actions sent her over the edge, her legs convulsing because of how strong her orgasm was. Micheal's pace stuttered, and he groaned, rubbing his cock against her clit, covering it with his spendings, and feeling his cock twitch against her. Sighing, she looked up at him and saw that he was leaning down, and his tongue was on her and in her. He pulled back, a satisfied look on his face.

"I knew you would taste good," he said as he went to get up off the bed. Willow got up in a sitting position and stopped him, kissing him until she was breathless.

"I... I don't know what to say, but god that felt good."

"I know, and if we do that until you're ready, I'm more than ok with that cause god was that hot," he said, pulling away from her with a kiss on her forehead.

"Now you need to let me go, little firecracker, so that I can clean myself up and you afterward," he said, as Willow moved back, not realizing she had both of his shoulders in a tight grip, which she let go a second later, as she laid back down in the sheets with a content sigh. Hearing the bathroom sink start-up as her mind was in the post-orgasm mode and smiling at her usage of what she only assumed would now be Micheal's nickname for her.

"Wait, did that count as sex or not?" she asked aloud in a quiet voice.

"That's on you. You were the one with the dating rule, not me," Micheal responded next to her as he got back into bed, damp washcloth in hand.

"Crap, I didn't realize that I said that out loud."

Micheal shrugged his shoulders and started to gently clean her as she grimaced against the feeling as he smiled. Throwing the washcloth onto the nightstand and moving her to be laid perpendicular to the bed frame, lifting her ankles to his shoulders.

"I think there's a better solution to cleaning you," he said simply, before his head disappeared from between her legs, leaving her a jolty shaky mess, and thinking back to it the next morning when she woke up cuddled next to him in bed.

Willow's thoughts were about the previous night's activities, as she stared at said man that brought her to the brink more than once. He was sitting opposite her. His focus was on the menu that was looking at. A server stopping at their table brought her thoughts back to the task at hand.

Her eyes scanned the menu, opting for a salad to go along with her ice tea. She handed the menu back to the server, and one ankle over the other. She opted to go back to the apartment and change as Micheal waited for her. The weather was so nice out; she wore a simple dress and some sandals. Her thoughts were still on the night before, completely focused on drinking some of her ice tea to distract herself. Which meant that she missed what Micheal ordered. He looked at her from across the table, putting his arms on the table and leaning his face against his hands.

"So I see your thoughts are elsewhere. I'm guessing you are thinking about last night when my face was level with your—"

"Nope, we aren't talking about that here. Out in public, what are you thinking about?" Willow responded, feeling her face heat at the thought of someone nearby hearing what he was trying to talk about.

"Oh, just wondering what you're into. I mean, you were into what we did last night multiple times," he said, sitting back in the chair, feeling his eyes go up and down her flushed form.

"Because the little make-out session by the pier was hot, maybe you would be down to do that again?" He said, making her think about that, feeling the ghost of his lips all over her. Willow's face heated as she crossed her legs one over the other to stop the heat that seemed to pool at his words—and seeing him smirk from across the table at her reaction.

"Can we change the subject, please? I don't think we should talk about something else," she said, sighing in relief when the server came over with the plates of food, placing the salad in front of her and then a plate of tacos in front of Micheal.

As Willow narrowed her eyes at his choice of food.

"Really? Tacos? Tacos?"

"What? Now you're reading into my food choice? I wanted tacos. There's nothing to read into that," he said as he squeezed lime over the Asada tacos and then put a generous amount of salsa on them.

Willow rolled her eyes, smiling and stabbing at her salad, taking a bite of it. Her eyes were going to his lips immediately.

Her thoughts were going into the gutter as she tried to focus on eating her salad, and he smiled at her.

"Well, that didn't take too long. You realize you have a big old tell of your face going completely red when you think inappropriately, right?" He questioned, putting the taco back down on the plate and taking a sip of his drink.

"Well, it would help if your lips weren't so...."

"So?"

"Just there and distracting," she mumbled, stabbing her fork into her salad and taking a bite as she crossed one leg over the other in order to distract herself from her thoughts.

"You think my mouth is distracting, just wait until my fingers come into play," he said with a wink as Willow groaned from across the table at him, as he chuckled.

"Remember how I said I would wind you up? The first date? This is exactly that if you were wondering," Micheal said, watching as Willow gritted her teeth at him, and was trying hard to not smile at his response.

"Oh, just eat your damn tacos please," she said as he quietly laughed at her frustration.

"Well, I have a surprise for you," Micheal says, breaking the silence.

"I highly doubt I'll be surprised. I think I saw everything last night anyway," she said with a knowing smile as he smirked at her, both leaving the restaurant arm in arm back to the car.Willow gets into the passenger seat as Micheal gets into the driver's seat, his hand brushing up against her leg that was crossed over her knee. She moved her leg back from his touch, as his eyes connected with hers, as he smirked at her. He was moving to click his seatbelt into place and starting up the car.

Leaving Willow wondering exactly what Micheal had up his sleeve. Until after a couple turned up a hill, they stopped over an outlook of the town. Willow smiled at the gesture and looked over at Micheal. Who was busy unclipping his seatbelt and placing his hand on her knee.

"I know you think I stopped up here for the nice scenery, but the gentleman in me is pretty much non-existent," he said honestly, as Willow felt his thumb rub circles along with her knee.

"Is this your plan? Cause from my knowledge this is how at lot of horror movies start out," She questioned, moving her legs to the side, and in doing so, moving Micheal's fingers from her leg as he sat up straighter and took a breath. He was running a hand through his hair and looking out at the scenery.

He laughed at her comment and leaned closer, his lips almost touching her ear as he said "well that might be true, it would have to probably be night time and its in fact daytime sweetheart," he said as he moved away a second later.

"I'm trying to control myself, but you in that dress," he says turning to look at her, and it looks as if he's just holding onto a thread of control, his hands were balled into fists at his sides, and his eyes were boring into her with the heat in them. Willow shifts her dress to cover more of her legs as she looks at him calmly.

"Alright, then I guess we can talk. I have to tell you I'm nervous about this. I know I set the rules and everything, but now that was the fourth date and everything. There are expectations," Willow said, feeling his hand go under her chin so she could look at him.The heat that was in his eyes a second ago was gone.

"Just cause I tell you I'm at the end of my ropes for waiting doesn't mean I still won't wait until you're ready. Screw the fact that maybe it was the 4th date just now. How about we talk about something, like since you weren't feeling too comfortable talking about us at the restaurant and everything? What are your preferences?" He asked in a calm voice that made Willow lean back a bit.

"You want to know about my preferences? Like sex?" She asked, blinking repeatedly, trying to wrap her head around how it got to this.

"Well, I feel like we both need to know. I would like to be prepared," he said as she felt his hand on her shoulder, his thumb caressing her shoulder as she smiled at him.

"You know you do that a lot, the thumb thing," she said as Micheal smiled.

"I guess I do it and I don't realize it is bothering you?"

"No, it's just nice," she said, leaning over the center console and pulling him to her.

"And I would like that elsewhere," she said in a husky tone, grabbing his shirt in her hands. Feeling his hands go to the back of her head, their lips coming into contact with each other. Then his hands moved from the back of her head to tilt it back, his lips lightly coming into contact with her skin, as he stopped and looked at her breathless form, as her skin was slightly pink from being worked up.

"So should I go in the back of the car first or you? Cause I can't exactly do what I want to with this console in the way," He stated, as he nipped at her earlobe and she moaned.

Micheal moved up from over the console to give Willow room to move, watching him run his hand through his hair again, noticing a slight pinkish tint that graced his face.

"Good thing I'm not the only one that's affected," she said with a laugh.

Instead of going out the side door, she leaped over the console and into the backseat, leaving Micheal to look at her, that same heated gaze on her again, as he smirked at her. Moving not as nimbly over the console as he tried to stop from falling on her with his hands on the backseat, resulting in both their chests touching and them laughing.

Willow looked up at Micheal, a smile still on her face, as he moved her red hair to behind her ear and looked down at her. And then something changed in his face, as he moved to sit in the backseat, running a hand over his face.

"We shouldn't do this even if I really want it to happen," he said as Willow pulled his hand from his face.

"I'm not a virgin. I think we both know that. And you were the one that said that the gentlemanly side of you was barely even existent anymore from having to wait?"

"Yeah, I know, it's just, I don't want it to be like this with you in the back of my car. It should be special, you know? I think my hormones were just getting the best of me," he said with a shake of his head and opening the back door and getting out. Holding out his hand for her to take.

Once she got outside, she smiled, turning and pushing him against the car, her hands traveling across his chest, feeling the muscles underneath his black t-shirt as she leaned up on her toes, pulling him down to kiss her.

"I understand you want to wait, and for it to be special. I want that too. That doesn't mean we can't have a little fun before then, though, cause you got me all worked up over lunch, so are you going to help me or am I going to help myself?" She asked, seeing the switch in his eyes to that heated look again, as he had his hand in his hair and licked his lips. Pushing her back toward the open door, her back hitting the plush cushion of the seat.

Having to lean on her elbows to look at him on his knees outside the car and taking her sandals off slowly, his mouth leaving a trail up one leg and then stopping just where her dress ended. And starting up that trail of kisses up the other leg. And then, holding eye contact with her as he moved her dress up to expose more of her legs to him, as he moved in closer to her. Placing her legs on both his shoulders. His thumb caressing her through her lacy underwear as he hummed.

"Guess you weren't lying about getting worked up at lunch. You're so wet," he said as he pulled her underwear from her. Making a point of slowly balling them up and placing them in his back pocket of his jeans.

Willow bit her lip to keep herself from moaning as she felt his fingers go right back to her. His thumb circling over her clit as she tried to move away from the contact. But Micheal's arm moving over her waist stopped her from moving.

"Ah ah, you aren't getting out of this until you've cum on my tongue, sweetheart," he said, his lips on her, licking her. Feeling him groan against her as she moaned, feeling his tongue flick against her clit in a circular motion. And then Micheal's fingers were on her, in her thrusting in slowly, one at first and then adding another one after waiting a second.

"God, you taste so good, babe," he said as Willow moved her legs around his head, bringing him closer to her as he smirked at her, working quickly. His fingers twisting inside of her as the combination of his fingers working her over and his tongue on her clit made her fall over the edge of pleasure.

"Yes, babe, cum on my fingers. I want to feel you," he said, pumping his fingers quicker. Willow's legs convulsed around Micheal's shoulders until she slumped against the cushions, sighing contently. Feeling his fingers leave her, as she looked up, seeing him lick his fingers clean and then placing a kiss against her clit, making her jolt from the oversensitivity. Putting her dress over her legs again and getting up from where he was kneeling.

"God, who needs dessert when I have you," he said as he took her hand in his, helping her stand up on wobbly legs as he chuckled, holding her against him. She could feel his erection rub against her as her hand trailed down the front of him. He stopped her hand, kissing her knuckles.

"You don't have to. That was just as much about you as it was for me too," Micheal said, kissing her before parting when his cell phone rang. He stepped back, rolling his dark brown eyes as he answered the call.

"Yes, Vic, I know about the premiere tonight. I was just going to get something new to wear. I know. Alright, see you tonight," he said, quickly clicking off the call.

"That was Vic, calling to remind me about the premiere, which reminded me of the real surprise, so we better get going," he said, a smile on his face, as went to open the passenger side door for Willow to get in as she stopped, holding her hand out.

"Can I please have my underwear?" Micheal narrowed his eyes at her question and smirked.

"I think I'll keep those as a consolation prize for how well lunch went today, don't you think?" He asked rhetorically as Willow groaned, not objecting to it. And got in the car, as Micheal smiled the entire drive to the next destination

TWELVE

"How am I not surprised?" Willow said as she was standing outside a lingerie store with Micheal next to her, all smiles.

"Well, I thought since I have the premiere, you could be my plus one. Which requires certain things," Micheal said as he opened the door for her as she walked in.

"You say that when I think you would rather I wear nothing at all, under anything that you would have in mind for this premiere. Since I have been assuming you wanted me to go with you tonight for it?" Willow questioned playfully, seeing the smirk on his face before she started looking at things and grabbing a few, but then stopped.

"Since this was a surprise, I'm assuming you have something for me to wear or I'm buying something. What exactly would the dress be? Since that's contingent on what I end up getting?" Willow asked as Micheal smiled.

"Oh, this isn't just for the premiere," he said with a knowing smile.

"Bet Pam loved when you did this for her," Willow said,

immediately regretting the sentence at the look on Micheal's face falling at the mention of his ex-wife—sending Willow's heart rate into overdrive and her thoughts. She quickly took what was in her hands already and went to a changing room. Putting the lingerie on the hooks and then grabbing for her phone and dialing.

"Hey, it's Willow,"

"Hey, what's up? How was the date? Or are you on it now and need an out? I'll give you an out?" Amanda questioned, hearing the rapid breathing on Willow's end.

"I put my foot in my mouth. we were flirting at this lingerie store-"

"Oh lingerie store, do tell! Are you guys getting stuff for tonight, like is this your foreplay shopping for lingerie?" Amanda questioned, as Willow could hear her friend's smile in her voice.

"No, I put my foot in my mouth, everything was going well, and then I just mentioned Pam, and I ruined the entire mood."

"Ok, well, where are you?"

"In a dressing room talking to you. God, I just know he's going to up and leave. I just know it," Willow said as she started pacing.

"Take a breather and try on stuff if you have anything. And then try to blow it off. Remember, sweetie. He's probably going to be way more forgiving with stuff like that. And who hasn't put their foot in their mouth at one point, right?"

"Yeah, but has anyone in mid-flirt mentioned 'oh ha, I wonder if Pam liked it when you took her to places like this?' Hmm?" Willow questioned, hearing her friend sighed on the other end.

"Just don't focus on it. I'm sure he isn't sitting there overreacting. Just take a few calming breaths and just do like I say. Try on some of the stuff and put it in the back of your mind. Plus, if you give him a little peek at the merchandise, I'm sure that'll settle any thoughts you're having too. Now, I do have to get back to work. But please give me details about the premiere," Amanda said as Willow smiled.

"Ah, Eric, told you?"

"Of course, he's going to be there with you, but I need things from your perspective, not just his," Amanda said, as Willow smiled.

"Fine. I'll tell you everything when it's over. Have fun at work, and I'll talk to you later," Willow said as she hung up the phone and turned to face the hooks that had various lingerie that she had picked up right before she made her stupid comment.

"I'm trying not to lose it right now," Willow heard from Micheal as she opened the curtain to reveal herself wearing a lingerie set of a pretty see-through set with the lace at certain parts to remain still. Her thoughts were going to him being pissed at the comment that she made. But she did not want to think like that, as Amanda said.

"Can you repeat I couldn't hear you?"

"I said that I'm trying not to lose it right now," he said, but Willow didn't see the smirk that was on Micheal's face as he looked her up and down.

"Oh, so then just leave if you don't want to see me anymore," she replied, seeing the look on Micheal's face at her comment, as he rushed forward to the dressing room and pulled the curtain behind him, to give them some privacy.

"No I, ugh. Ok, it would help if you calmed down. And just look at me, ok? Do you feel anything at all? That might show something like, oh, I don't know. A breeze, perhaps?" He questions with a big smile on his face as Willow looks down and sees that she is only wearing the lingerie, her thoughts so narrowed in on leaving the shop she forgot.

"Ah! I almost walked out in this," she said, as she went to grab the dress that she came in wearing and pushed Micheal out, who was laughing.

"Mind you, if it were just me and not an entire store full of customers and employees, I wouldn't have complained. But I don't think you would have wanted to be confused as someone trying to steal merchandise," Michael said from behind the curtain, clearly laughing about the situation. Willow was changing from the lingerie she wore and back into her underwear and bra and the dress she came in wearing and, slipping on the sandals back onto her feet, stepping out of the dressing room with the lingerie on the hangers with a smile on her face.

"I mean, I have to get it now from the look that was on your face. If this was the surprise you were talking about coming here, then it was a pleasant surprise," Willow said as she walked up to the counter to pay for them. The previous emotions that she felt were forgotten as she saw Micheal smile at her before walking to the main entrance waiting for her to buy the items in hand. And she was then walking out arm-in-arm as he took the bag from her hand.

"So we go to a lingerie store. Now what? You told Vic that you were picking something up."

"Yeah, something new for myself and something for you as well," he said as Willow grimaced internally.

"What? Did you get a measuring tape at night and take my measurements?"

"No, not like that. I got a dress of yours via Amanda and got the measurements from that. Since this was about a week ago, I got everything together. They planned this a month in advance, so having you as a plus one of mine was a kind of last minute.

But Vic could work things out," Micheal said as he drove in the house's direction.

"So not only a dress but jewelry?" Willow said as Micheal rolled his eyes.

"Yeah, but it goes together, don't overthink now. I think you need to be dotted on," he said, as he walked into the walk-in closet, coming out with a gown in a protective covering that was in a hangar.

"I still can't believe you got me a gown. I mean, it's one thing to rent something, but this is a custom gown you realize–"

"What did I say? Don't overthink it. This is technically the fourth date, and I want to take my girlfriend out to this premiere and show her off. And I need to talk about things for the next gallery showing tour that I have to talk about." Micheal said, opening up the protective covering, revealing a glittering silver gown. With simple straps,

"Try it on. I hope it fits," he said as he passed the hangar to her. She took the dress with her, walked into the walk-in closet, set the dress on one dresser, and looked at it. She grimaced, trying not to get her head into that space of overthinking the kind gesture of him getting her a dress for the premiere for her. But she couldn't help but think with this being the fourth date, just like she mentioned, held certain expectations.

"How is it going in there? Need me to zip you up?" She heard from outside where Micheal was waiting—making Willow move to grab the dress, take it off the hangar, and then place it back on the dresser, trying to take calming breaths.

"Stop overthinking. It's just a dress. Put it on and see if it fits and then go from there," she mumbled as she quickly stripped off the dress that she had been wearing and made quick work of putting on the silver dress. Fixing the straps around her shoulders, putting her hair back behind her shoulders, and walking out of the closet.

"Yeah, you are going to have to help zip me up," she said as she turned to face away from him. She was feeling his fingers on her back as he zipped the zipper up in her dress. Hands were moving to her shoulders and turning her to face him.

"I want to see your face, not just your ass in the dress, even if it's a nice ass," he said as he smirked down at her, moving her red curly hair from her face and back behind her shoulders. Micheal took a step back and looked at her.

"So do I look like a garbage can with a nice dress on or?"his eyebrows furrowed at that comment.

"What's with the self-deprecating humor? You look great," he said, as his hands were still on her shoulders, rubbing soothing circles on her skin.

"Because I'm the last-minute plus one that is going to be amongst all these hot celebrities and rich people and–"

"You are beautiful, and your beauty is real. Most people that will be there are fake, literally made of plastic. Use their money to create a version of themselves because they aren't happy with what they saw in the mirror, so they used their mass amounts of wealth to boost their egos. Trust me, I'll be a very proud boyfriend with you on my arm," he said as his hands moved to Willow's face, placing them on either side of her face.

"Yeah, well, can you put that on repeat until we are there? Maybe that'll help with my anxiety over all of this," she replied.

"Well, if it makes you feel any better, misery loves company. You're not the only one that's anxious about this," he said as he took a couple of breaths.

"But you know that I'm worried that those people are going to ask about the attack since Vic tried to squash some things about it. But not all of it." He said as he turned around, not facing her and noticing his hands shaking.

"Ok, well, just keep the conversation to your art. It would surprise me too, you know, to think they would take the time to ask questions. But I'll be there for moral support," Willow said as she took one of his hands in hers, squeezing it.

"Yes, thankfully. And Vic will be there to help as well if I need him. Unless he goes, the 'even bad press is good press thing.'" Micheal said, giving her an uneasy smile.

"Ok, well, how about this? I think this comes with matching shoes. Because I can't imagine walking around barefoot on a red carpet for a movie premiere?" she questioned, trying to get Micheal's attentions off the thoughts that were nagging at him.

"Yeah, and I forgot to show you the jewelry as well," he said, a smile on his face as he wiggled his eyebrows at her.

"Well, then I'm also going to say that before this premiere that I'm going to want to see you in that suit of yours. Which will be the first time seeing you in a suit, so that'll be something," she said as he smirked.

"Oh, because you're going to jump my bones later? Right?" he said as they both laughed.

"Maybe, it's still up in the air after all. After tonight we might just need some stress and tension relief," she said, sitting on the bed, waiting for Micheal to go grab the rest of the things that went with her outfit and his suit as well.

Willow readjusted her dress. She was feeling the heavy fabric in her hands and having it fall back into place. Looking down at the red carpet that she was standing on, moving her high-heeled feet against the carpet. She was feeling the roughness of the mat against the bottom of her heels.

It was a distraction, a distraction from the camera that was flashing as she felt Micheal's hand moving against her waist, pulling her closer to him. Regarding his hand that was on her side, and felt it shake slightly against her.

"You ok?" she asked, plastering a smile on her face for the cameras. Hearing him take a deep breath in and out and feeling his hand stop shaking after a second.

"I'm good. It's just nerves," he said reassuringly.

Just out of frame from the red carpet, there Vic stood, as if he appeared out of nowhere. And he was looking happily at them, a smile on his face as he walked up to them just after they walked the red carpet.

"So, you two clean up nicely," he said, adjusting one ring on his fingers before hugging Micheal.

"You know, if we had a crystal ball back then, I don't think I would've imagined us like this. You with your art and me being the one that manages you."

"Yeah, well, you're one that contacted me years ago at my start, not the other way around, you know?"

Vic looked down at his phone, a look coming across his face that Micheal couldn't read as Vic pulled away from him.

"I just need a second. You go to your girl, go have fun," Vic said as he went to text on his phone furiously.

They both walked out of the premiere, hand in hand, feeling the warmth of Micheal's hand in hers.

"So why is it that this is the first time that I don't feel excited about a movie? I just feel relieved that it's over."

"Oh, trust me, I'm the same. Usually, these events are more enjoyable, and I thought bringing you along might help me, which it did. I think if you weren't with me at the beginning, I would've bolted after walking the red carpet."

Seeing that Vic and Eric were standing off to the side, talking furiously back and forth, making Willow feel like there was something brewing. Since Eric and Vic kept on pointing at Vic's phone. Micheal walked up to them as Eric took steps away from them and walked up to Willow, plastering a smile on his face.

"What was that all about?"

"Oh, you know, he can't get away from his phone, pissed that I wasn't working on work during the premiere," Eric said, shrugging his shoulders, a smirk plastered on his face.

"I mean, I'm working right now, which is funny, considering I know who else is working hard right now, if you know what I mean."

Willow felt her face heat at his comment, knowing what he was talking about because Amanda said she would hear about the premiere from Eric. Amanda and Tommy were absent. Which could only mean what his comment meant was about Amanda and Tommy.

"Ew, that's my best friend you're talking about Eric, just ew," she said, smacking Eric's shoulder as he laughed at her reaction.

"Was I talking about your friend?" He questioned, as Willow smacked his arm again.

"God, what did I bring Amanda into, I swear."

"Well, you didn't bring her into anything more so Tommy would be into—" he said as she interrupted him, by putting her hand over his mouth as she felt him laughing and pulling away.

"I hope you have fun, Willow," he said as he looked over at Vic and Micheal, as Micheal turned away from Vic, looking royally pissed.

"I'm done talking to you," he said as he took a couple steps away from Vic and started walking away, as Willow hurried to catch up with Micheal, as he put his arm around her waist.

"So, what is up? What happened?" Willow said, looking from Micheal to Vic, who was talking now furiously with Eric, who was also shocked as Vic had a minute ago.

"Nothing, let's go. I had a surprise that I think would be very good to go off to right about now. I think we both need a break from all of this," he said, gesturing to the red carpet and where the press was standing a couple of hours before the movie premiere.

"Ok, well before that, you think we could swing by a place and get some food? Cause I'm starving," Willow said as he squeezed her hand, smiling. All ounces of tension were gone from his face.

"Yeah, food would help right now," he said as they walked off to the car that was waiting for them—getting inside and directing the driver towards a drive-thru.

***

Getting out of the car, fast food bags in hand, Micheal gave the driver money.

"No, no, you don't need to," the man said as Micheal shook his head.

"Take it, as a tip for waiting and dealing with everything," Micheal said before following behind Willow and getting out of the car too. Watching as it drove off from the property, leaving Willow and Micheal standing outside the house entrance.

"Come on, the longer that we sit here, the colder this gets, and that means the less edible sadly," she said, waving one bag that was in her hand, making Micheal fish through his pockets for his keys faster—and unlocking the door.

Once inside, Willow took her heels off with a sigh at the front door. She was going to sit on the couch. Micheal toed off his dress shoes, undid his tie, and joined Willow on the couch as she passed him a paper-wrapped item. As she dug into the fries.

"This is exactly what I needed after tonight," Willow said as Micheal laughed before taking a bite of his burger.

"Why does it taste so good? Like, I don't think I've had fast food that's tasted this good before? And I've had a lot, considering, well, Evan and everything," he said as Willow smiled.

"Because we are dead tired, so anything is going to taste amazing. But that's not what I'm wondering about. I've been pondering the surprise you mentioned. Is it just a quiet night here because I don't care? That sounds pretty nice if it's just that?"

"No, something more, but surprise. So, I'm going to be keeping it close to the vest, of course,"he said as he looked at her with a smile on his face.

"But it requires packing if that helps," he said, finishing his burger in two bites before stealing a fry from Willow and getting up and walking out of the living room.

"Hey, ok, that was a hint, but what am I supposed to pack? I have nothing unless you're counting the stuff from what I left here from before," Willow said, following Micheal up the stairs to the master bedroom, where he walked into the closet, grabbing two suitcases and placing them on the bed. Which made Willow narrow her eyes skeptically.

"You planned this,"

"Um, of course, I did. That's how surprises work. They are planned," he said as Willow rolled her eyes.

"So besides the stuff that was left here, I mean, how long is this trip supposed to be? Cause I only had enough stuff for a weekend."

"Yeah, it's for this weekend, and what you have would work," he said as Willow paid attention to what he was putting in his suitcase as swim trunks went into his suitcase. Along with jeans, shorts and a couple of t-shirts.

"That would all work, plus some things that you picked out today, of course," he said with a knowing smile. Micheal quickly zipped up his suitcase and went to unzip Willow's. Her suitcase was already packed with everything before Amanda packed for that fateful weekend when the attack occurred. Plus some lingerie pieces that she bought today.

"You packed for me already, ok," she said, trying not to over-think this romantic gesture Micheal was going for.

"Yeah, since I knew what you would need because I know where we are headed," he said, re-zipping the suitcase.

"But I think we are going to want to change before we leave," he said as he looked down at himself and then at Willow as she nodded.

"Agreeing with you on that," she said, turning her back to him, so he could help unzip her as she slipped out the dress, letting it fall to the ground. She was turning to face him, biting her lip at the sudden feeling of anticipation as he looked into her eyes. Then shook his head.

"I'm going to go change into something that doesn't feel like a mild form of torture," he said, loosen his tie until it came off, grabbing a t-shirt and sweats from his dresser.

"No kidding," she said, laughing as she smiled, shaking her head as she grabbed shorts and a t-shirt to change into. She was trying to shake that anticipation, feeling coursing through her body at the thought of the place they would go to and other things on her mind.

Thirteen

"So we have everything packed? Now, are you going to tell me where we are going?" Willow asked, putting her suitcase in the back of the suburban.

"That would ruin the surprised look on your face when we get there, so no," Micheal replied with a smile as he got into the driver's seat and turned the ignition on. Sliding an ice chest closer to them that was in the back seat that was stock full of drinks. As well as a bag that was next to it full of snacks, so they wouldn't have to stop anywhere since it was so late at night.

"Fine, have it your way, but if I say 'are we there yet?' repeatedly you're the one to blame," Willow said as she got into the passenger seat and buckled her seat belt.

Two hours in and Willow was shifting in her seat, trying to fight back the tired, as Micheal leaned back towards the ice chest and grabbed a water bottle, and threw it at her. As the condensation around the bottle contacted her skin, she jumped in her seat.

"God, you might have well just poured the water on me,"

"Good point, I'll do that next time then," he said as he adjusted his hands on the steering wheel and smirked at her, as he turned up the air. Making it blast harder on her face.

"Water, air conditioning, you're trying to keep me awake, huh? If you keep at it with the water bottles, we are really going to stop at a rest stop," she said, as she unscrewed the cap and drank from it regardless of her statement.

Because he had a point. Staying hydrated would help, and she wouldn't be able to fall asleep on him with a full bladder.She squirmed in her seat, as Micheal smiled at her in her peripheral vision.

"So, where are we going? Since you need me to stay awake and everything?"

"That would ruin the surprise, but I want you to stay awake. There is something coming up that will let you know where we are," he said as Willow grabbed her phone in her pocket.

"What are you doing?"

"Just wanted to call Amanda to let her know where I'm going unless you don't want me to?" She asked, trying to shake the ever-familiar feeling of being on guard that Andrew left her with.

"No, no, it's not like that. I just thought we could have a no phone kinda weekend, you know? Dead to the world?" He said as he held her hand and squeezed it.

"Does this have something to do with what happened at the movie premiere? Because Vic was nice before and then was so different afterward. Something happened, didn't it?"

"It's nothing, he's just overreacting, it's in his job description as my agent."

"Ok, well, that doesn't explain, Eric, though. I don't think I've ever seen that man angry until tonight. Care to explain that away?" She questioned, hoping that he would drop just a hint at what happened, and what he was clearly avoiding by taking her out on this spontaneous trip so late at night.

"It's nothing, I promise you that. Overreacting over media stuff, that's all," he said, patting her hand and smiling at her.

"How about we listen to some music, huh? It'll keep you awake," he said as he turned on the radio as Turn Up The Radio by Autograph came on. Willow watched as he hummed along with the song and drummed his fingers against the steering wheel before turning to look out into the darkness of the highway. Her thoughts are going on tonight.

There was a sense of excitement and anticipation within her at that thought, since they had waited so long. For her to be comfortable, considering her past with Andrew. And she did it because she didn't want to jump into bed with the first guy that showed her just an ounce of attention and then regretting it later. Which was why she stipulated the 4 dates, which he could've made quicker, she realized, if he really was just interested in having sex with her. But he didn't. He considered her situation and agreed to wait. Although they both kind of slipped up in their last little intimate moment, that was more of a tension release than anything for the both of them.

She was anxious, excited, and nervous about tonight. Worried that at the last second, she would crumble and over-think it and stop it. And she didn't want to stop it, considering how attentive he had been to her this afternoon in the car. That memory brought up a smile to her face, feeling her face heat at the thought of his lips on her again.

She closed her legs, feeling the air conditioning on them, as she grimaced at the poor choice it had been to wear pajama short bottoms in the car. She had wanted to be comfortable, but now it was causing issues.

"You ok over there?"

Willow looked over at him in the darkness and saw him smiling at her as he continued the drive.

"Yeah, just thinking about things, that's all,"

"Well, it's coming up soon, just round this bend," Micheal said as Willow sat up in the seat, craning her neck as they rounded a turn on the highway. And then there were lights. But not really lights at all. But a row of distinctive buildings that were lit up in a rainbow of colors along a river.The Colorado River. Willow realized as a smile crept up her face as she realized where he had brought her. She fist collided with Micheal's shoulder playfully as she laughed.

"Are you kidding me? Laughlin? This was your surprise? I love it! This is exactly what we needed!" She said excitedly, kissing the side of his face enthusiastically, as he chuckled at her reaction.

"Yeah, well, it's even better, actually. Because we are staying at a house of mine that I have out here. Right on the water," he said as Willow was sitting straighter in her seat as they got closer and closer to the exit on the freeway.

"Just because you have a place, well, can we still go to the casinos? I haven't been here in years." She said as Micheal smiled.

"Of course, I know there are some lounges in them. We could go to them to do some dancing tomorrow?" He offered, taking the exit and driving through the town. All the while, Willow was looking out the passenger side window, excitement written all over her face.

"I hope you packed sunscreen cause you're going to need it when we are out on the boat tomorrow," he said as he turned into a gate community typing in the gate code to unlock the gate and drove a bit until he turned into a driveway. Micheal turned off the car and went to grab their bags in the back. With Willow getting out of the car and staring at the house.

It was a dark brown, almost tan, two-story building. Illuminated by lights set up in the very desert-friendly succulents and scrubs next to the driveway. Walking alongside Micheal he opened the front door and flipped on all the lights. An expansive living room with a flat-screen television mounted on the wall. A kitchen with dark marble counters and an island. Her eyes scanned the house as she followed Micheal to the stairs. Going up and turning a corner where the master bedroom was located. With a four-poster bed that had a soft headboard against the wall. Which made her roll her eyes, all the mental images coming into her mind with that headboard. As Micheal set both of the bags down.

"Do you want to take a bath or shower? Just cause I know it's a bit of a change,"

"Oh, you mean the dry heat that feels like a blow-dryer to the face, but it's your entire body? Yeah, I'll be thinking about that," she said, fanning her tank top against her to create a breeze in the slight hothouse.

"I'm going to go turn on the central air. It could be a few minutes before it gets cold," Micheal said as he walked out of the master bedroom, leaving Willow alone.

She opened up her suitcase and put her clothes inside a dresser. Then opened up Micheal's putting his clothes away for him in the other dresser, her fingers going around one item that felt like a box. She took it out of the bag, finding a box of condoms that had her face heated, but then she quickly put the box in the top drawer of his dresser.

"Oh, you didn't have to — "Micheal said, stopping as he looked down at Willow kneeling by the suitcase looking at the object in her hand.

"Before your mind goes further into the gutter, I wanted to give you a tour of the place, well the other side of the house that looks out to the river," he said as Willow dropped the box on what was now his dresser with a heated look at him before following behind him.

———

"How about a drink, out on the balcony we can talk," Micheal said, as Willow almost thought she saw relief in his eyes as the thought came to him, as he went into the fridge and grabbed a chilled bottle of wine. And watching as his eyes scanned the cabinets, trying to remember where the glasses were and opening one and grabbing two wine glasses.

They walked back up to the master bedroom, where there was a sliding door and a balcony that overlooked the river. Micheal set the wine glasses on the ledge so he could open up the wine bottle. Micheal opened the wine bottle with an audible pop and poured some in each glass and then set the bottle down on the ledge next to the glasses.

"Hold on," he said as he walked over to the wall and flicked on a switch and little lights lit up the balcony in the darkness, as Willow smiled at him, picking up her wineglass and handing the other one to him. Sipping at it as she looked out at the river in thought.

"You know I've been thinking, and I have to thank you. I realize I've been more myself since I've been with you since," he said, sighing and taking a sip of his wine as he moved closer to Willow.

"What do you mean, more like yourself?" She questioned, turning to face him, wondering exactly what he was talking about.

"Well, I was like this before. Not questioning things I said or did. Not to really blame Pam. I know people do slightly change when being with someone for so long, but. I guess I got so used to certain things that I changed myself so that I wasn't happy with the person I would look into the mirror at. And I didn't realize until after the divorce how much I changed in the negative, I guess. That was until you came along. It was like a breath of fresh air. I can be more myself around you, and I want to thank you for that," he said as he wrapped his arm around her waist, pulling her closer to him as he looked down at her.

And she knew, she just knew, what was coming next. She could feel it. The dreaded L-word. She pulled away from him, downing her glass of wine, and smiled.

"How about you show me your dancing skills? See how you are before we go to the casino tomorrow tonight to go dancing," she said, resting her hands on his shoulders.

"Ok, it's been awhile though," he said, downing his glass of wine, before turning to her.

"Wait, we don't have music, I can go get my phone," she says, moving away from him and towards the master bedroom where her bag is that has her cellphone inside of it. He pulled her back against him, stopping her movements.

"I don't think we need music," he said, moving one of her hands to his shoulder and the other to his hand. His other hand landed on her waist, pulling her closer to him as they started swaying slowly together.

"This is a first, me slow dancing in my pajamas," she said, moving to rest her head against his chest, as she heard him humming something under his breath.

"Are you humming Led Zeppelin?" She questioned, as she picked up the tune, as she moved to look up at him, and he smiled down at her.

"Well, you said you thought you needed music, plus it relaxes me," he said, turning the both of them around on the balcony, as he spun her out with calculated movements as she smiled, before spinning slowly back into him.

"I guess I can say I've slowly danced in my pajamas and to

Led Zeppelin now," she said absentmindedly as he went back to sway back and forth with her in his arms.

"Yeah, I guess we both can say that now," he said, holding her against him, as they swayed to him, humming Led Zeppelin as Willow joined along with him.

FOURTEEN

Willow woke up the next morning. The sunlight peeking in through the blinds of the master bedroom. Pulling the covers over her head, Willow felt around her body for a second and felt her pajamas on her from the previous night. Giving her a clear hint that nothing happened the previous night.

She tried to think back to the night; it was hazy after coming into the house. The house tour and then going out to the balcony. And then the alcohol. She turned over in bed, grimacing against the sunlight and moving up on her arms to go for the blinds to close them even further to have the bedroom doused in darkness so she could go back to sleep.

The arm that wrapped around her suddenly scared her as she jumped slightly at the contact and looked over her shoulder, seeing Micheal slightly awake behind narrowed eyes and his mushed up hair from sleep.

"What are you doing?" His voice even sounded heavy with sleep as he pulled her closer to him.

"Just trying to make the room darker. I think we both hit the bottle pretty hard last night, so we might as well sleep in a bit more,"

"Bottles," Micheal corrected, groaning out the answer.

"What?"

"I think you mean bottles plural. Started out with one and then I think we drank three between the two of us," he said with a grimace on his face at the memory. Willow turned to face him, her head sharing the same pillow as she noticed something on his face.

"What?"

"You have something..." she trailed off as she moved his face to the side and started laughing.

"Well, I guess we did drink. You have part of a cork stuck on the side of your face," Willow said, taking it off Micheal's face, as holding it out to him as he rolled his eyes, tossing it in the trash can that was next to the bed.

"I don't remember how that got there. But that's not really much a surprise with us both being hammered last night. And don't think I didn't see you checking to see if you still had clothes on. I think it's a good thing it didn't come to that with being so drunk and everything. But that can be easily redeemed," he said as Willow looked up at him and saw the thoughts rolling through his head, as he fixed his hair that seemed to be everywhere from him moving around in his sleep.

"But I think before we even think about that we need coffee, and something to eat because I don't know about you, but it feels like I have someone playing the drums in my head. Remind me to not get us both or our own bottles of wine to drink when we want to have some wine before bed again," he said with a kiss to Willow's lips that was there and got in a second as he got up from bed. Hearing him walk into the kitchen and making the coffee up. With the scent of freshly brewed coffee wafting into the bedroom a minute later, with the sounds of the coffeemaker brewing.

Micheal came around the corner, leaning against the doorframe in only his boxers, giving Willow a view of his broad tan chest.

"Are you coming? Or am I going to be the only one drinking coffee this morning?"

After grumbling for a second, Willow got up, her eyes narrowed at him as he smiled at her.

"Yes, you definitely aren't a morning person," he said, chuckling to himself.

"No, before coffee I'm not," she said, going to the coffeemaker and pulling the carafe out and getting a coffee cup out, pouring a bit of the black coffee in it and sipping at it for a second and closing her eyes. Feeling his arms going around her waist, his head resting on her shoulder lightly.

"Better? Are you becoming more human by the second, I think I might see it actually," he said playfully before kissing her shoulder.

"Oh hush, I was already human. Just wakes me up, that's all,"

"Whatever you say, caffeine addict," Micheal said before going to grab pans and get eggs from the fridge.

"I was thinking French toast? Are you opposed to that idea?" He questioned, as he looked over his shoulder with the fridge door open, looking into it.

"No, not at all. It sounds great," she said with a smile, sitting on the kitchen island, intent on watching him make breakfast.

"You know what you need is a little tip jar. I mean coffee and a show, I'm pretty sure if you did that, while just wearing those boxers of yours you would probably make more money than you have with your paintings," Willow joked as Micheal was cracking eggs into a bowl and scrambling them.

"I'll tell Vic your idea, I'm sure that would amuse him," Micheal joked as he threw in some cinnamon and vanilla into the scrambled egg mixture, mixing it together.

Pushing the plate that had remnants of syrup on it away from her, Willow sighed.

"That was great. Or maybe I was really hungover and needed food, or both. I can't decide,"

"Well, I take it as a compliment. You eating all of it. But I guess I was hungry because I ate all my food as well," he said, grabbing both plates as putting them in the sink, not noticing the grimace on Willow's face.

"Yes, I'll eat the food and then I'll gain the weight and then you won't like me anymore, or find me attractive," Willow said, hopping off the bar stool.

"Wait, you really think that? That I would stop liking you because you were eating food? Because you have a hangover? I like you for you Willow, and I will not stop feeling that way," Micheal said, coming around and grabbing her hand to stop her.

"You're just saying that to appease me."

"Guess I'll just have to show you how much I care about you, huh?"

Willow gasped in surprise as his mouth covered hers, lifting her up on the counter. Her legs opened and wrapped around his waist. Lifting her up in his arms. Her hands going into his long hair, her lips moving to his neck, as he walked the both of them into the master bedroom. Setting her down on the bed, and then going to shut the curtains that lead out to the balcony.

Willow watched his fast movements as he went to his bag and saw that it was fully unpacked, as she laughed a bit at his expression on his face as he started looking through the pockets of the suitcase.

"They are in the top drawer of the dresser on the left," Willow said as she saw the frazzled, nervous look leave Micheal's face instantly as he opened the top drawer and a look of relief replaced it.

"Ok good, cause I was getting it in my head we would have to do what we did last time. And yes, it satisfied us both, I know. But I don't think that would be enough this time," he said, getting up and turning to face her with the foil packet in his hand on the nightstand, smiling at her, a look of realization came over him as he went to his other bag.

One that Willow had not seen before rifling through it and coming out with a little bag pouch that had white ties. A smirk on his face as he turned to face her.

"Now where was I? Oh yes, now I have to prove to you just how you make me feel, by making you feel good," he said, going to lie down next to her. Setting the pouch between them both. One of his hands trailing up and down Willow's arm, causing goosebumps to rise to the surface. Micheal leaned over and kissed her softly, one of his hands cradling the back of her head as Willow moaned into the kiss, feeling his tongue go in her mouth. Feeling his fingers go to the straps of her tank top, as her hands were fisted in his t-shirt, the material bunched up in her hands. He pulled away with a slow sigh, leaving his lips as he licked them.

"I want you," he said, his fingers rubbing circles into her shoulders as she sat up.

"And I want you, naked though," she said as she went to pull him up in a sitting position, and took his shirt from her hands and moved his shirt up, revealing his chiseled chest.

"Alright, alright you're taking no for an answer," he said, chuckling as he went to get up from the bed and take off his shirt. Willow did the same thing, but fumbled, feeling her hands shake slightly as she pulled her tank top over her and off. Leaving her in just her pajama shorts and bra.

"I'll be the one to take over from here," Micheal said, Willow's eyes scanning, taking in his form that was only covered by boxers now.

His hands on her shoulders, pushing her back to lie on the bed, his fingers flicking the back of her bra, unhooking it as he slipped it from her arms. His fingers went to her nipples, rolling them between his fingers until they were raised peaks. Then lightly pinching them as Willow moaned, feeling his tongue replace his fingers on one of them. Sucking on her nipple before lightly nipping at it. Blowing on the sensitive bud, leading to more heat pooling in her lower belly. As his hand was kneading her other breast with his hand. Then her other nipple got the same attention from his mouth.

Trailed his mouth up through the valley between her breasts to sucking on the side of her neck and nipping at it. Before leaning his weight on his hands and looking down at her and kissing her. Willow felt his hands go to her pajama shorts waistband, feeling the air conditioning in the room make everywhere he had touched more cold. And then she felt between her legs, and the wetness there. Even through her pajama shorts as she groaned, seeing him rest his weight on his ankles, looking down at her with a wicked grin on his face. His fingers moved from the waistband to the seam on her shorts, feeling the wet fabric.

"I guess someone is wetter than I thought they were, huh?" He asked, not really wanting an answer, as Willow moved her legs wider as he chuckled.

"I guess we should have a rule while we are here, no more underwear for you, you'll just ruin them all," he said as Willow felt his fingers go to her waistband again, pulling the shorts from her, along with the underwear, flinging the both to the floor leaving her bare to him. His fingers trailed up and down her legs lazily, taking in the goosebumps that soon covered both her legs at the sensation. Until they stopped at her inner thigh.

Thinking that his fingers were going to her clit, she tensed up and felt his hand leave her inner thigh. And He picked up the pouch with one hand, untying the ties, and taking out what was inside and in Willow's line of sight. His other hand rested softly across her hips to hold her in place. Willow furrowed her brows, trying to think of what it was. It was on the tip of her tongue, on what it was. Until he clicked on a button on it and it started vibrating. He smirked at her, taking the toy in his hand and lightly pressing it against her clit. Her hips jolted at the vibration. Feeling him moving the end of the device in circles on her.

"I thought you were wet before I took off those panties of yours, but look at you now," his voice was full of wonder and appreciation.

He clicked the toy through the various modes, and put it back on her clit, feeling the low vibration affect her. Feeling herself get wetter. His other fingers holding her open, watching her get wetter and wetter under his gaze.

"If I would've known how wet you get from me just looking at you, ugh. I can't wait to feel how wet you are when I'm inside you," he said, moving his hips against the bed. Making Willow groan because this was affecting him as much as it was here, from the very clear erection he was sporting under his boxers.

"I want you," she groaned, only hearing the click of the warning before feeling the vibration on her clit start up faster, making her thrash around on the bed, as he chuckled.

"Not yet, sweetheart. I want to see you cum first, then I'll be inside of you, don't you worry," he said, leaning down and kissing her quickly, and then clicking the vibrator again. Making Willow's hips want to leave the bed, but he was holding them down, as she felt more heat pool in her lower belly. As she tried to roll her hips against the toy.

"God yes, that's so hot, watching you try to get yourself off on the vibrator baby," he said, as his words sent her over the edge, leaving her a shaking mess underneath him. Feeling the vibrator go over her sensitive clit as she tried to pull away from it. And then the click and it was off and he moved to put it on the nightstand, and then the sound of the foil wrapper being opened. Willow moved her head to the side, seeing him taking off his boxers and rolling the condom on himself before settling himself over her. His hand trailing up and down her side, and looking down at her with a smile.

"You do not know how sexy that was watching you cum. Now I know you get off on my voice, that'll be useful," he said, leaning down and kissing her slowly, lazily, as if he wasn't sporting an erection and waiting for her to come down from her orgasm.

He moved down her body again, leaving another wet trail of kisses down her body, stopping at her inner thighs, nipping at both of them. Causing her to reflexively open her legs wider. She looked down at him and felt his warm fan over her, then his tongue was on her, inside her just for a second, before it was gone and he kissed her clit before raising up again. Willow looked up at him and saw that his lips were wet as he licked his lips clean.

"Sorry I just had to taste you before," he said as he took his dick in his hand, running it over her pussy, slowly, making Willow groan, waiting for him to be inside her. Because she realized that what he had done before wouldn't be enough, not anymore.

"Please, I want-" She said as she cut her plea off in a groan as he slowly thrusted inside her, stopping until he was fully seated inside of her.His forehead rested against hers just for a second as he was over her, waiting for her to adjust to him. Willow smiled, leaning up to kiss the side of his face, as she brought her legs to wrap around his waist, bringing him closer to her, as he groaned over her.Rolling his hips a bit, Willow moaned at the sensation as he slowly started thrusting in and out of her.

"God, you 're such a good girl you know that," he said, as Willow nodded at his words. Not realizing until now how much his voice affected her as she felt heat rise in her at his words. She closed her eyes, lost in the sensations, as she tried to match his rhythm. That was until he switched it up and started going faster. Thrusting in and out of her at a brutal pace.

"God yes, I can feel you squeezing me babe, I want to feel you cum on my dick babe," he said as Willow groaned at his words, until she felt his hand go to her clit rubbing it in circles, sending shock waves throughout her body.

"God yes, you 're close aren't you babe? cum for me, cum for me," he chanted as Willow's back arched and she was moaning his name, her hands gripping onto his back. A few seconds later, his rhythm became out of sync and he was groaning over her, feeling his hips pump himself inside of her as he came. Feeling him leave her, and roll onto his side and discard the condom in the trash can. And then Micheal was back on the bed a second later lying on his side and pulling her to him. Willow was too tired to even open her eyes, but she heard his rapid heartbeat in her ear as she laid her head on his chest more than satisfied.

"That was.." she said, at a loss for words.

"Worth the wait? I know it was," he said as he kissed the top of her head as she started dozing away.

"I'll let you rest, but fair warning I'm not done with you," Micheal said, a possessive tone in his voice, as Willow smiled.

"Give me 15 minutes, then I'll show you just how much I'm not done with you just yet," she said, hearing a groan from him as the only answer as she closed her eyes.

FIFTEEN

Willow rolled over in bed, smiling. Feeling more happy than she ever did before.

"Wow, and I honestly was nervous about all that. I still can't believe I was," she said as Micheal rolled on his side.

"Hey, I was nervous too, you know? But I think we just worked through all that. And this did kinda help," he said, grabbing something on the nightstand and waving the little blue item in his hand.

"I guess, but can you get that vibrator out of my face?" She said, pushing his arm away as he laughed.

"Why? You liked it in other places?" He questioned, turning it on and running it over her exposed shoulder. The vibration, making her move away from it, as she batted it away. Feeling her face heat.

And then the vibration was gone.

"Alright, it's gone. But you know I'm still going to make you more comfortable about that, since I know you need other stimulation. Which I'm more than willing to use that for. Especially if it makes you—"

"Yeah yeah I know. Some girls need that. Maybe I do. I just, can we not talk about that? It's ruining my orgasm buzz," she says, grabbing for him as he laughs, moving over her and pressing his mouth quickly over hers before he's off the bed.

"Fine, I'll leave you with your buzz. I'm going to go down and see what else we have in the kitchen,"

Willow moved up in a sitting position and watched as he put his boxers back on as she hastily got out of bed. The sheets tangled around her leg, as she saw the entire bedroom tilt at an angle. Until a pair of warm hands grabbed her, pulling her up before she could even blink, and put her on the bed.

"Thank you," she said clutching at her naked chest, as Micheal patted her shoulder as he leaned down, grabbing his shirt and handing it to her.

"Yeah, well, I didn't want a repeat of you on those school steps again. I think a sprained ankle would definitely ruin the trip vibes. Or at least probably confine us to only certain positions, and I don't want that," he said, leaning down to kiss the side of her face before walking out of the room and down to where the kitchen was. The sound of opening cabinets is the only telling sign. Willow took his shirt that was in her hands and put it on and followed him shortly into the kitchen. She rounded the corner and saw him looking into cabinets, giving her a great view of his back and other assets. Her eyes glued to him, as he turned at the sound of her feet with a smirk on his face.

"Are you enjoying the view?" he questioned in a low tone.

"Sorry, I think I have to take a minute to turn my brain back on, because of the multiple orgasms and just that, all of that," she said gesturing to his form, as he laughed, turning around to face her, a bag of chips in his hands.

"You're thinking about eating again? Cause I was thinking

about other things," she questioned as an idea came to her that made her smile at him.

"Oh, I know that look," he said as he threw the bag of chips back into the cabinet.

"Well, I said, what, 15 minutes? And since this is my first time here and everything," she said, trailing off as she took a step closer and started running her fingers up and down his arm. Just like how he did to her. Looking up at him, she saw his face go blank once her fingers came into contact with his skin, as he leaned against the counter, effectively banging his head against the open cabinet. Completely ruining the moment.

His answering hiss in pain, and one of hands going to the back of his head to rub the affected area of his head, made her stop her ministrations.

"Are you ok?" she tried to ask, trying to keep her voice neutral but wanted to laugh.

"Yeah fine, just a stupid reminder to close the cabinets, I guess," he joked, as he turned to close all the cabinets. As Willow looked over at the living room with the tv, and the plush couch and went to sit down on it. Turning on the remote and flicking through the channels. The added weight of Micheal sitting next to her minutes later and his arm wrapped around her shoulders was her only warning.

"So you were saying? Before I stupidly ruined the moment?" He questioned, making Willow.

"Oh, you wouldn't be interested in it at all," she dismissed, watching in her peripheral vision as his eyes narrowed, but there was a smile on his face.

"Try me," he challenged.

"Well, there is the entire issue of multiple rooms that we need to break-in and I was thinking about the couch," turning to look at Micheal and he's smirking.

"I do like the way you think, but I have to get a couple of things first. Hold on," he said as he got up from the couch, in a non-rushed way. Until he was away from the living room and she could hear him running up to the master bedroom, leaving her shaking her head and grabbing the remote and changing the channel.

Willow pulled Micheal down closer to her, moaning into the kiss. He pulled away, gripping his cock in his hand, leaning over her as he guided it to her entrance. Willow watched the look of concentration come over his face. That was broken in a second just as he was entering her, as she moaned. His hand covering her mouth to muffle her moan, as he stopped over her.

"Shh, I think there's someone out in front of the house," he said as he looked over the couch that they were both sprawled out across.

Willow looked up at him and saw his eyes scanning the front entrance. And a second later, a look of relief washed over him as he removed his hand from over her mouth. He leaned down and kissed her again as he swiveled his hips, moving himself deeper in her.

"Thank god, I would hate for anyone to ruin this," she said just as the sound of keys in the doorknob were heard and the door was opened.

"Hey Micheal, just—" was heard from the doorway, as Micheal groaned in frustration, moving his body to cover Willow. Grabbing for a nearby blanket to cover her with as she peered over the couch and saw Eric, Tommy and Amanda standing in the doorway. Eric was quick to put his hand over Amanda's eyes, as Eric and Tommy averted their eyes. Leaving

Willow scrambling underneath Micheal to get away, just as he moved out of her. As she ran toward the nearest bathroom, a blanket covering her naked form. With Amanda shielding her eyes and going to follow Willow.

"Congrats, Willow, I knew you could do it!" She shouted, running toward where Willow ran off to.

Sixteen

Leaving Tommy, Eric alone, Micheal was putting on his boxers quickly, while his friends' backs were turning.

"Oh hey, well, look at that. See, when he said he would come down and work on the place, I didn't think he actually was. But look at that, crown molding," Tommy said as Eric laughed, hitting Tommy's shoulder.

"Uh huh, crown molding, didn't think I could ever say at all that I was walking in on one of my friends doing his girl and seeing his O face. Now that's burned into my brain. Just burned, scarred really,"

"Ok, that's enough. You can say all the jokes you want around me, but you can't when Willow gets back. But what I really want to know is why the hell are you even here?"

Eric and Tommy gave him wary looks.

"Guess you haven't heard, huh? We kinda came to warn you," Eric said as he cleared his throat.

Willow ran off into the first bathroom that she could find, hearing footsteps following right behind her.

"I knew you could do it. I knew you could get back on the horse. Even though technically Micheal was the horse. But I'm splitting hairs here," Amanda's voice carried across the walls.

Willow's hand turned the knob and pushed the door open and closed it. Just as a hand came to stop the movement, resulting in her opening the door to a smirking Amanda.

"So you guys finally had sex. How was it?"

"Well, you just walked in on us. Don't really want to talk about it. I want to take a shower and never leave this bathroom," Willow said as she closed the door and started up the shower, dropping the blanket that she had been clutching around her form. Stepping into the warm shower and closing the curtain behind her.

"You know you can't wash the shame away, right?" Amanda's voice said from behind the door.

"I can try, can't I?" she countered, grabbing for body wash and rubbing it all over her, finding herself wanting Micheal there right then with her. Except they were so rudely interrupted.

"Well, maybe next time put a sock on the front doorknob? How were we supposed to know you guys were otherwise occupied exploring each other's bodies? No less on the couch,"

Willow groaned at her friend's response, knowing she said that thought aloud, placing her forehead on the cool tiles as the warm water cascaded over her. Trying to get her mind off of the looks of shock on their faces as they walked in.

"You know you were the one that ran, Micheal didn't. He covered you when he could've covered himself. Isn't it just refreshing to be with someone that isn't afraid of their body?" Amanda mused, making Willow smile, since it sounded like Amanda was speaking from experience.

"Speaking of how it is with those two?" She asked, getting to work on washing her hair. Since she was in the shower, she might as well actually get herself cleaned up.

"Oh no. I'm not spilling anything. This has to be mutual. You tell me some details, I'll tell you some. That's how it goes,"

"Fine," Willow said as she turned off the shower and went to open the curtain. and a hand emerged from the other side of the bathroom, towel in hand.

"When did you get in here?"

"You always have so many questions. A minute ago. Now, get that towel on so we can talk," Amanda said, impatience clearly in her voice, as Willow wrapped the towel around herself and rang out her red hair before moving the shower curtain to the side and stepping out onto the bath mat.

"Alright you want details, you follow me," Willow said as she exited the bathroom and walked in the direction of the master bedroom, passing the front room where Eric and Tommy were talking to Micheal in low tones. She didn't look in the direction of the living room, but felt his eyes on her. Entering the master bedroom, Amanda let out a whistle as her eyes scanned the expansive room and went right out to the balcony to look out at the view.

"This is really nice, you know that," she said, leaning over the railing and looking out at the river.

"Oh, I know, we drank wine out there last night," she said, going for her dresser and picking out a two-piece bathing suit to wear underneath a white t-shirt and denim shorts. Taking a peek over her shoulder, she saw Amanda was still looking out at the view and Willow changed quickly into the bathing suit.

"So other than drinking wine out here, anything else happen out here?" Amanda said as Willow turned to face her as she was putting her t-shirt over her head, not missing the wiggling of Amanda's eyebrows suggestively.

"No, that all happened this morning. We got way too drunk last night. We woke up with hangovers-" Willow said as she saw a look of surprise cross her friend's face as she walked into the bedroom briskly and over to the side.

"And this?" She questioned, picking something up. Willow's face heated up as she took the few steps in front of Amanda, grabbing the toy from her friend's hand.

"I can't believe you actually picked it up, and yes, this. He packed it. Not me," Willow said defensively, making Amanda shrug her shoulders.

"Doesn't matter who did, just that you enjoyed yourself, in my opinion. As long as you did, I wouldn't judge what you both do together in private. Now I'm going to go wash my hands since I touched it," making the heat on Willow's face recede at her friend's honesty.

"Yeah, you should go do that," as the toy was placed in her hands, her thoughts going back to just earlier that morning with a slight smile on her face, as the sound of running water took her out of her thoughts, looking up and seeing Amanda sidestep the sink with the water still running.

"You're definitely going to have to clean that," nodding towards the sink, making Willow roll her eyes.

"Yes, yes, I know," Willow said as she walked up to the sink, washing it in the hand soap under the warm water, grabbing a hand towel and wiping it dry. Making sure to look at Amanda pointedly.

"Happy? It's clean now, not that I wasn't going to or Micheal wasn't going to. We just got carried away, that's all," she said as she walked back to the nightstand, grabbing the black pouch and putting the toy in it, and cinched the bag closed and put it in the nightstand drawer. Turning back around and seeing Amanda watch her with a smile.

"What?"

"Oh nothing, just that you wouldn't have done that when it came to Andrew, or at least acted this way,"

"What way am I acting?" Willow asked, feeling like there was going to be some judgment coming from her friend.

"Confident and sexy as hell, that's what. Which makes me feel bad that we barged in on the two of you. Sorry about that. But we did try to call at multiple points this morning to get ahold of you guys," Willow felt the heat on her face return, hearing about their multiple attempts at contact.

"I guess we really did get distracted, even the phone here?"

"Yep, that too, but again, don't feel ashamed about it. I wouldn't be. Which reminds me," Amanda said as she marched out of the master bedroom, Willow following shortly behind her friend. And seeing the straight shoulders of her friend, knowing that she was meaning business as she walked back into the living room, all three men were still talking together and turned to look at her.

"If any of you bring this up, me or Willow get total permission to throw your ass overboard in the boat," Amanda said, turning on her heel and walking into the kitchen and opening up the cabinets. As Willow followed, trying to not laugh at the comically scared expressions on all three men's faces at Amanda's genuine threat.

"Oh orange juice, wait, I have a good idea, I'm sure there's, ah ha!" Amanda shouted triumphantly as she was opening up multiple cabinets in the kitchen and found a bottle of champagne.

"I'm making mimosas. Who wants one?"

The only answers being slight groans from the men in the living room. And then the sound of the television being turned on and Micheal was walking in the direction of the master bedroom, winking at Willow as she blushed in response, hearing the shower started up again in the bathroom.

"Hey, stop being in dreamland missy and help me get glasses arranged," Amanda said as she was getting the blender out to mix the orange juice and champagne together.

"God, you and a pointy knife to open that thing," Willow said, staring at the Champagne bottle, watching Amanda look in one drawer and pulling out a butcher knife to pop the cork with.

"Please, ye have little faith in me, remember New Year? We survived then. What makes this any different?" She said as she held the bottle away from her and angled the knife against the cork as it popped off with a loud noise, foam flowing from the top. Willow tried to tip the bottle back up so the foam wouldn't get all over the kitchen floor as Amanda poured a generous amount in the blender and then equal parts of orange juice.

"Would it still be a mimosa if we added blended ice to it? Or would that make it a margarita?"

"I think you mean frozen mimosa actually," Willow corrected as Amanda threw in a good portion of ice into the blender before throwing the top and hitting the switch as the mixture of Champagne and orange juice combined with the ice.

Sitting and drinking out on the patio, Willow and Amanda clinked their glasses together as they watched as Micheal, Eric and Tommy were taking the boat from where it had been parked in the back and out onto the water. It was a slow process but it was enough to entertain the two women seeing Eric sitting in the boat as Tommy was helping Micheal navigate the boat down the ramp and out into the water.

"Maybe we should've held off the drinks before they started doing this," Willow cringing at the mental image that she had of them ending up with both the boat and the suburban in the river.

"Well Micheal didn't drink. He's the designated driver tonight."

"What are you talking about?"

"Oh, when you were in the bathroom I heard Micheal say that you guys had plans to go out tonight. Go out to the casino, have dinner, go dancing, maybe some gambling too?" Amanda said, before taking a sip of her drink. As Willow thought about it, and tried to control her facial expression, and saw Amanda's smile fall.

"Or we can get our own plans and not crash yours. I totally get it. We've already kinda crashed your weekend. I wouldn't want to impose anymore than we already have," she said, nodding her head in an understanding way, but it also made Willow feel guilt creep up.

"No, no, you guys can definitely come. Why wouldn't you? Plus, it'll be fun since I haven't really spent that much time with Eric and Tommy, anyway. I mean, you have spent more time with them than I have," Willow said with a smile, placing her hand on her friend's shoulder, giving it a reassuring squeeze.

"Plus, I want to see if they are approved by me anyway. Yes they are Micheal's friends but you never know, you know?"

"Hey! You guys want to go out on the boat? Cause we are going to go out to dock it up for tomorrow?" Eric yelled up at them as they both smiled at each other.

"Um of course we wanna go out just tie it off to the dock so we can all get ready and pack an ice chest," Amanda yelled back down as Eric nodded relaying the message to Micheal and Tommy as both girls down the rest of their drinks and then ran off to their respective rooms to change into their bathing suits.

Willow looked at her reflection in the mirror, trying to fix the straps of her two piece bathing suit. It was a tankini top and shorts combo that was comfortable enough. And was happy that it had been packed because she thought she spotted an inflatable tube and wanted to be prepared if they were going to take turns being towed in it behind the boat.

She was adjusting the straps that were twisted around, just as Micheal came up behind her. Wearing just gray swim trunks and nothing else, he slipped his fingers underneath her straps to fix them.

"You know if they hadn't crashed this weekend I think we would be in one of the other rooms by now,"

"Or the patio, or the boat actually," Willow continued with a smile directed at him through the mirror as he smirked back at her.

"The boat?"

"Oh, you have no idea what you've awakened?"

"A sleeping giant with a big pointy stick?" Micheal joked as Willow turned around to face him, laughing.

"Did you really just quote history to me? Albeit you mixed up some things. But don't be quoting presidents quotes when it came to the United States during wars in an attempt to flirt. Even if it was kinda funny," Willow said as her fingers found their way to the ties that were on the front of his swim trunks.

"Good to know, no quoting history to the history major if I don't know it down pat," he said, running his fingers through her hair, pulling away from him to grab a hair tie and put her hair up in a simple ponytail that made her red hair pouf out even more.

"Oh, it's not that. Actually misquoting to me is kind of funny, don't stop on my account. Just don't use it to flirt, cause let me tell you I'm anything but a sleeping giant with a pointy stick, I think that technically more you than me," she said checking her hair in the mirror as she felt him leaning into her. Resting his lower region against her on purpose as she smiled.

"See, I told you, pointy stick," she joked as he rolled his eyes.

"I wouldn't call it that more—" he said when he was interrupted by the bedroom door opening, revealing Amanda with Eric trying to stop her from opening the door, as he tried dragging her away. Her hands bracing the doorframe in an attempt for him to not drag her away from the master bedroom.

"Ice chest is packed, if you two don't get your butts down in like a minute we are stealing the boat!" Amanda said cheerfully, as she backed away from the doorframe and left Eric standing there dumbfounded, as his eyes followed her movement.

"God, she's bossy," he said as he looked at the two of them.

"But yeah, she's telling the truth. We are so stealing it, if you don't make it down in like a minute or two since we are all ready to go and everything," Eric said before leaving them alone again.

Willow shook her head at her friend as she started walking out of the master bedroom, feeling Micheal's hand grab at her wrist.

"You know I really don't think they would miss us,"

"Yeah but I really want to go out on the river, so more alone time is just going to wait," Willow said, patting the hand that was on her wrist, as he let it go and followed her out of the house and towards the dock where the boat was tied off to. Willow got into the passenger seat that was next to the driver's seat. Smiling at Amanda as she sat in the back of the boat between Tommy and Eric.

Coming back into the house two hours later, Willow felt the effects of the sun as she practically had to drag herself into the house. As Eric and Tommy passed her with the ice chest, setting it down outside on the patio before going into the house.

"I don't know if I'll be able to make it to the casinos tonight. I'm so tired,"

"Well, take a nap, excuses are for quitters," Amanda said, walking past her, going to the fridge to grab water with a smile on her face. Before going to join the boys out on the patio, passing by Willow.

"I know what you're doing. Trying to play tired so you don't go out and then that means that Micheal won't go out either and then it's back to fun times here," Amanda said, emphasizing what she was saying with a thrust of her hips.Willow felt her face heat at that.

"Yeah, I have to admit that would have happened but I'm honestly so tired right now I don't think I'll make it to dinner or dancing tonight I'm afraid," she said, going to lie down on the couch and grabbing for the remote and flicking through the channels. Feeling Amanda's eyes on her the entire time.

"Uh huh, keep up the excuses Willow, doesn't mean we can't drag you there, anyway. Take a nap for a bit," Amanda said before walking out to the patio, where they were playing music and drinking.Micheal came into the house, his eyes scanning the living room until they landed on her, with a sympathetic look on his face.

"You know you're going to end up with a sunburn tomorrow or maybe even later. Probably why you're so tired right now from the sun exposure," he said as he walked into the kitchen, grabbing a washcloth and running it under the water before ringing it out a bit. Joining her on the couch and holding it out for her to take.

"This will help, trust me," he said as Willow took the washcloth and pressed it to her neck, closing her eyes at the cool sensation of feeling it help combat the feeling of tiredness that she was feeling.

"Well, maybe I shouldn't have drank that many beers either,"

"You only drank like three,"

"Your talking to someone that stupidly wanted to do bodyshots off of you and then admitted to being a lightweight. Trust me, it's the combination of alcohol and sun that aren't mixing right now," she said as she leaned her head against Micheal's shoulder as he took the remote from her and started flicking through channels, stopping at a random movie.

"You really should listen to Amanda, though. Take a nap and see how you are after that and drink some water. You should be good as new," he said as Willow closed her eyes, succumbing to the tiredness that wracked her body.

SEVENTEEN

Amanda had been right. An hour later, Willow was up and feeling better, just as everyone was getting ready to leave to go to the casinos for dinner and dancing. Willow got up off the couch and went to the master bedroom and looked through her suitcase.

Finding a halter top dress that was something she knew Micheal packed to prepare for going out for dinner. She changed into it, slipping the halter top closure over her neck and staring at her reflection in the mirror. Hoping that the sunburn wouldn't make it look like she was a human version of a red glow stick.

Taking into consideration her curly red hair, it made the sunburn not look as bad. And the lines of the halter top fell within the same as the swimsuit lines, which helped in making it so her shoulders didn't have horrendous sunburn lines.

Running her fingers through her hair, she turned to put her feet into her pair of very worn sandals that were her favorites to wear. Thankfully, Micheal was mindful of packing the dress because of the warm humid weather. She put a bit of mascara on and a light touch of pink lipstick, stepping out of the bedroom ready to leave with everyone else.

Seeing everyone else out in the living room, doing last-minute touches in the mirrors. Eric and Tommy were talking to Micheal by the door.They were all dressed casually, just like her; the men wearing t-shirts and jeans. And Amanda was also wearing a flowing little black dress and sandals.

"So ready to go?" Micheal asked, looking at everyone and waiting for some type of objection from anyone in the group.

"Actually, hold on," Amanda said, holding up a finger before leaving them and walking back into the kitchen. All that could be heard was a cabinet opening and glass sounding on a counter. With her coming back into the living room trying to keep a hold of four shot glasses full of clear liquid.

"I only grabbed four because I know you wanted to drive," Amanda said, nodding at Micheal as she passed a shot glass to Eric, Tommy and then Willow.

"To having a fun night tonight!" Amanda shouted, as they all clinked their glasses together and took the shot, each one of them wincing at the harshness of the tequila.

"That's one way to start the night," Eric said, shaking his head as he handed his glass back to Amanda, taking each glass from everyone and depositing them into the sink.

"Alright, now we can go," she said, as Micheal shook his head, opening the front door. Clicking the remote to the SUV to unlock it. They all piled in. Amanda sitting in between Eric and Tommy in the back and Willow up on the passenger seat next to Micheal. As Willow leaned against the seat to give Amanda a knowing look at her, which Amanda rolled her eyes at playfully as they all clicked their seatbelts into place.

Seeing the lights of the casinos made Willow giddy as they got closer to them. She hadn't been out here in years. This time, however, was with a different group that was highly unpredictable. Willow had seen Eric and Tommy a handful of times before, and they seemed calm enough. But adding Amanda into the mix with them and she knew she would bring sides out of them that no one rarely even saw. Which with how Willow perceived how the two older men were around just her, and not how they could be with just Amanda. She knew they were only going to be trouble. Adding in Amanda and some alcohol. Willow knew that this night was going to be quite interesting for sure.

"So what's the plan for tonight, exactly?" Amanda asked as she popped her head from behind the driver and passenger front seat of the vehicle.

"Well, like I said before. Dinner, dancing and maybe a little gambling," Micheal said as he stopped in the parking lot.

"And here I thought you would've thrown in something else,"

"Yes, but see you kind of crashed this trip, so," Willow said, feeling annoyed since the trip was just supposed to be them. Having Amanda around was nice. But the plans were originally set up for just the two of them, not a group.

"How about we do our own thing for a bit and meet up later?" Tommy suggested as he opened up his door and Eric did the same, as Willow heard them all exit before closing the doors. And seeing Amanda walking in between Tommy and Eric, looking back and giving Willow an apologetic look.

And then she turned in her seat and looked at Micheal. And he was looking right back at her, a neutral expression on his face.

"I guess someone else is annoyed too, I take it?"

"Oh, you were with this, too? I thought I was the only one," Willow said, relieved.

"Well, I would have let them tag along. But I did just want time for us. Since that's what this entire trip was about. Eric and Tommy can be fun to hang around, but they can be a lot sometimes."

"And we wonder how Amanda ended up with them, huh?" Willow questioned rhetorically as they laughed, getting out of the SUV, as Micheal held out his arm for Willow to take as they walked into one casino and up to where the restaurants were a couple floors up.

Walking hand in hand out of the restaurant, Willow and Micheal stopped right outside of it. Micheal pulled his phone out of his pocket to check and see if he got any messages from either of the guys.

"They text you to let you know where we should meet them?" Willow asked as he clicked off his phone.

"Yeah, they are on the bottom floor. Dance lounge," he said with a groan.

"Sounds like someone doesn't want to go, but they are expecting us. So, let's go, mister, get your dancing mojo flowing," Willow said as she took his hand as she walked in the escalator's direction.

"See, I would rather have the drinks flowing than the dancing mojo having to flow," he complained lightly, but Willow could hear the smile on his face.

"Hey, we had a little time to ourselves. And they had time for themselves. And yes, they kind of crashed this trip. But I think it's for the best if we just go with it, you know. Plus, they aren't really that bad," Willow said as they made their way over to the dance lounge, hearing the music pouring out of the open doors.

They both stopped as they looked out onto the dance floor, their eyes scanning through the crowd trying to spot Tommy, Eric, and Amanda in the flashing lights and the swaying bodies.

Micheal took hold of Willow's hand more firmly as he led the way through the crowd, with Willow walking right behind him. The both of them sidestepped people all the way to the bar, where Micheal pulled out a chair for Willow to sit on.

"See them anywhere? Maybe they aren't here and out playing some—" Willow said, stopping mid-sentence as her eyes locked onto a trio that was out on the dance floor. They were hard to miss with the dancing that they were doing, or more like grinding to the beat of the music.

"There they are, right there!" Willow shouted over the music to Micheal as he turned to see where she was looking and spotted them. She could tell because of the shaking of his head. Willow slipped off the barstool, her feet on the floor once again as she followed right behind Micheal, keeping her hand on his shoulder as they walked towards Eric, Tommy and Amanda.

"I can't believe what I'm seeing," Willow said, more to herself out loud as Micheal stopped walking and she stopped just before running into his back, and went to stand beside him.

"Seriously?" Willow questioned, as Amanda's eyes locked with hers and she stopped dancing in between both men. Causing both Tommy and Eric to look at her and then to where Amanda was looking at. Which was right at Micheal and Willow.

"Well, it is a dance club. What were you expecting us to do? Sit in a booth and drink?" Eric asked sarcastically towards Willow and Micheal.

Willow was trying to come up with an answer as Micheal just shook his head.

"Just didn't think I would ever see one of you dance like

that, that's all," Micheal said, patting Eric's back, as Willow smiled.

"Yeah, I've seen you dance but never like that," Willow said, smiling as she noticed her friend's hardened expression on her face as she stepped away.

"I'm just going to go get a drink and I'll be back," Amanda said as Willow looked at the three men. Knowing that Amanda was thinking something else entirely about Willow's response to the dancing.

"I'm going to go too. Anyone want anything?" She asked, glancing in between each of the men in the group.

"Water would be great actually," Tommy commented as Willow nodded, and noticed Eric elbowing Tommy in the side.

"You make yourself sound so old asking for water dude,"

"Well, I don't know about you, but I need some water after dancing under the lights." Tommy said as Willow heard their bantering get lost in the music's sound that was playing in the club. As she worked her way through the crowd to where the bar was. Spotting Amanda as she was leaning against it, waiting for her drink.

"Five waters please," Willow said to the bartender that came around. She knew everyone would need some. Especially her and Micheal from the amount of wine they drank at dinner. And from what Tommy hinted at, she could only guess that they went straight to the dance club after parting ways with them earlier.

"Hey, you know I'm not assuming things with you, right?" Willow asked, turning to Amanda, seeing her friend's hardened expression at her once again.

"What do you mean? The judgmental look on your face as you walked up to us dancing or when you snapped at me earlier in the car? Or is it both?" She questioned, grabbing for her drink as soon as the bartender passed it to her. Taking a long sip of it.

"I wasn't judging you. Not really. It was more surprising to see you dancing with both of them like that. Those are moves I haven't seen in a while, that's all. And earlier in the car. I just, this trip was just supposed to be a break for Micheal and I. Because of the press lately. I know you didn't intend on crashing or anything,"

"But we are totally cock-blocking you right now?" Amanda questioned, with a slight smile on her face as she sipped at her drink.

"Just a little. But that's totally fine, you know. Having you guys around is fun and everything. And getting to know more about those two is interesting, of course," Willow answered honestly, feeling the weight of it lift from her shoulders with being able to tell her friend exactly how she felt about the situation.

"Yeah, I kind of would be, too. I'll mention it to them. We can always leave."

"No, no. Stay. You are already here and it is fun with you guys. Plus, the trip is only for a couple more days, anyway. Might as well stay," Willow said, patting Amanda's hand, just as the bartender came up with the five cups of water. Giving a tip to the bartender, Willow grabbing two and Amanda grabbing the remaining three.

"Shall we get back to them?"

"Yes, we shall. Let's see if they convinced Micheal to dance. That's something I haven't seen really yet," Willow said as they both laughed while walking through the crowd, holding their drinks over their heads as they walked until they got back to where Micheal, Eric and Tommy were standing in the middle of the dancing crowd.

"Here, get everyone some water," Willow said, handing one cup to Micheal and watched as everyone downed their cups quickly. Willow started drinking hers and tried to step up closer to the group, but couldn't. Feeling her sandal behind held down as the front strap broke as she stumbled forward. Looking down, she saw the strap completely broken on the sandal.

"Great, just great," Willow said, picking up her broken sandal.

"Ok, well, we can always find a gift shop here and get you another pair of sandals," Amanda offered.

"Yeah, in the meantime, I'm going to have to walk all over the hotel's flooring. Might as well cut it off," Willow said with a groan.

"I can take you," Amanda offered, as Willow stepped back as she looked over at Micheal, as he downed his water.

"We can go together and find some sandals," Micheal said as Amanda nodded.

"See you in a bit?" Amanda asked as Willow sighed.

"Yeah, maybe. I'll let you know. After walking with one foot around this place, you never know," Willow joked as she pulled out her phone to check the time.

"I'll text you if we come back. You never know if something might just come up," Willow said with a wink, causing Amanda to laugh at her friend's joke.

"Fine, but now you're making me think you broke that thing on purpose," she said as Willow hugged her, Eric and Tommy as Paul did the same.

"How about you text when you are done we can come back and pick you up?" Willow offered once she realized she would essentially leave them stranded out at the hotel since Micheal was the one that drove everyone out.

"Hey, it's fine. We can catch a cab to take us back," Eric said, waving them off.

"Go 'get those sandals from the gift shop'" Eric said, waving them off as he did air quotes, as Tommy and Amanda laughed next to him.

Micheal and Willow turned around and started walking out of the club, Willow hobbling along with only wearing one sandal on her tiptoes to get the smallest amount of her foot in contact with the plush carpeting that was throughout the hotel's ground floor.

"They really think you broke that on purpose," Micheal said as he took the sandal that was broken that was still in Willow's hand and threw it in the nearest trash can.

Willow took the other sandal off and threw it in as well, since there was no point in just keeping the one sandal.

"Yes, as if I did it on purpose, but I didn't. Someone stepped on the back of it as I was trying to step forward. But doesn't mean I will not use that as a way of getting out of that casino. Let them have their time together and let us have our time together," Willow said, as Micheal smirked at her and swiftly picked her up bridal style, causing her to laugh in surprise as they walked out of the casino and towards the SUV.

Eighteen

Willow woke up the next morning, tiptoeing around the house. Since she didn't know when Tommy Eric and Amanda got back from the casino after her and Micheal came back after breaking her sandal last night in the dance club.

"Still need to get new sandals," she said with a shake of her head, since instead of going to the hotel gift shop to buy a replacement pair, they both made it more of a priority to come back to the house since they knew they were going to be alone for a while.

Getting water, she filled up the coffeemaker and started putting grounds in. Pressing the on button, the percolating noises of the coffeemaker filled the air as Willow turned towards the kitchen sink with a grimace.

The mimosa glasses from last night weren't washed and after sitting overnight had an overpowering, almost fermented smell that made Willow gag as she ran the water. Filling the sink up with hot soapy water to cover up the smell as she started scrubbing away at the blender container and the glass cups from last night.

"At least it isn't puke, at least it isn't puke, ugh," Willow repeated as rinsed everything off and put the glass container of the blender and the glasses in the drying rack. And then washed her hands.

She opened up the cabinet above her and pulled out a coffee mug and set it on the counter next to the coffeemaker and went to the fridge to grab some coffee creamer. Opening the fridge, she leaned down to grab it and closed the door. Gasping in surprise as she clutched at her chest at Amanda standing right next to the fridge.

"You scared the crap out of me!"

Amanda looked at Willow with a raised brow and looked down at the ground.

"Think you are going to want to rephrase that, nor do I need to think about putting you in a senior home for voiding your bowels all over the floor because I scared you," Amanda said with a smirk on her face as she poured herself some coffee. Grabbing for the creamer and pouring a good amount of it, to the point the coffee could barely be categorized as coffee with how pale it had become in her mug. Willow shook her head at her friends' comment and also coffee drinking habits.

"So, when did you guys make it back here?" She said, then sipped at her coffee to distract herself from her raging hangover that was making her head pound.

"2am? Only because they had to close to clean and reopen the club in a couple of hours," Amanda said with a shrug of her shoulders.

"But tell me, was the sandal thing a ploy? Because you know you can tell me the truth? You shouldn't have to feel you have to make up reasons to go off and hookup with him," Amanda continued.

"Yes, Amanda, it did actually happen. And those were some of my favorite sandals. And I don't really have anything else. So I have to go shopping before we do anything else today," Willow said, watching as a smile creeped up on Amanda's face at the mention of shopping.

"Well, what are we waiting for? Let's get dressed and go! We can leave them here to nurse their hangovers and we can go see what's around here, just us girls," Amanda said downing her coffee quickly, and Willow sipped at hers, watching as Amanda went to get ready in the room that she was sharing with the boys.

"I will go wake up Micheal and ask him about it. I'm sure he'll just take the car."

"If not, we can always take Eric's that we drove here in, no big deal," Amanda said, popping her head from around the open door with keys in her hand. Willow shrugged her shoulders at that.

"Ok, then I can just go get ready. See you in a few," she said, as she walked up the stairs to the master bedroom. Going to flick on the lights, but stopping short, remembering that she should avoid waking up Micheal. Who was sprawled out on the bed under the covers, still sleeping.

Willow grabbed a t-shirt and jean shorts. Looking around on the floor, she spotted Micheal's sandals that she picked up since she spaced on grabbing another pair of shoes in case this exact thing happened. And walked into the bathroom to change, throwing her pajamas that she wore the night before on the hamper on the way out, tiptoeing out of the room. As Micheal stirred in his sleep and Willow freezed at the door. And looked back at him, waiting for his breathing to level out again.

"Mmm... I love you, Willow," she heard mumbling against the pillows, as she blinked. Thinking she was hearing things. Because he didn't just say the big L word in his sleep, right?

Willow closed the door softly behind her and walked down the stairs. Trying to get her mind out of the spinning, due to the fact that she just was lucky enough to catch before leaving, as she stopped at the end of the stairs and thought about her feelings about that simple set of words.

"Just leaving them a note, I managed to not wake them both up somehow," Amanda said, shaking Willow from her thoughts. Amanda laughed as she jingled the keys in her hand and they left the house, closing the door behind them softly.

———

Willow and Amanda walked back into the river house an hour later. They had bought new sandals and breakfast for everyone that they had picked up at the grocery store on their way back from getting the sandals. Setting down the container of the danish on the counter, Willow tore off the tags on the dollar sandals she found. And threw the tags away, as Amanda was opening up the danish container and looking at it, butter knife already poised to cut into it.

"Don't you think we should check on the guys? See if they are awake yet?" Willow questioned as Amanda shook her head.

"If the smell of coffee didn't wake them—" Amanda said as the sliding door that led out to the back part of the house opened. Eric, Tommy and Micheal walk through the door, already wearing their swim trunks.

"Ah back already and you brought breakfast," Eric said as he grabbed the knife from Amanda and cut out a section for himself, picking it up from the tray and taking a bite out of the small rectangular piece.

"How are you guys not looking like crap?" Amanda said, looking at all the guys, especially at Eric and Tommy. Which confirmed to Willow that they must've drunk a lot last night while they were out dancing.

"It's called hydrating, you know, drinking water," Eric replied, finishing the rest of the piece of his danish.

"Speaking of water, we got the boat all set up and thought we would go out for a couple of hours. Already packed the cooler and everything," Micheal said as Willow's eyes connected with his and he smiled at her.

Bringing what happened earlier back to the front of her head. The big L word, even in his sleep.

"Ah, yeah, why not?" Willow said, shrugging her shoulders, looking at Amanda, who was just walking toward her room that she was at with the boys.

"Already going to change. I'll be ready in a couple minutes!" Amanda shouted before closing the door behind her.

"Alright, guess I'll get ready too. I'll be down in a bit," Willow said as she walked upstairs and into the master bedroom, closing the door behind her and feeling her head spiraling at the thoughts that were going through her head at the thought of the big L word. Love. He said that he loved her. But did he really?

Getting on the boat, Willow opened up the ice chest. Rooting her hand through the ice and finding the beer and popping the tab open before she sat down in the seat that was next to Micheal, who was watching Eric and Tommy untying the ropes off the sides of the boat and pushing it away from the dock and out in the current.

They both walked past Micheal and Willow to sit in the back with Amanda in between the two of them.

"Anyone want anything?" Willow asked as she grabbed the

top of the ice chest to close it. Looking back at Amanda, Eric and Tommy, and then back again at Micheal.

"Water for me please," Micheal said, as Willow passed him a water bottle that he put into his cup holder that was next to the accelerator hand controls.

"Beer," Amanda, Eric and Tommy said as Willow threw them each a beer before closing the top of the ice chest. As Micheal turned up the gas on the boat and they were on their way to explore more of the river.

A few hours later and more than a couple beers consumed, everyone except Micheal. And they were on their way back to the river house to eat lunch. Willow could see the house in the near distance. Narrowing her eyes, she could make out the shape of someone that was sitting out on the front by the water, waiting impatiently under the shade of one tree.

She turned in her seat to grab another beer and caught the thin lipped expressions of all three men that were in the boat, Amanda oblivious to this and dancing in her seat as she drank her beer in the back, sitting in between Tommy and Eric.

Micheal slowed the boat as Tommy got up. Hurrying to the front of the boat and diving off it to get hold of the clip that was attached to the anchor. Connecting the clip to the front of the boat, Tommy grabbed the ice chest that Eric passed over to him. One by one, each of them got out of the boat, Amanda and Eric getting off the back way, submerged in water up to their waists.

Willow got up from her seat, grabbing her sandals as Micheal took the key out of the ignition, and grabbed for his own sandals, his face still showing little emotion.

They both walked up to the front, Micheal hopping off first and then Willow went to sit on the edge of the boat, and looked down at the water. Knowing that the water would certainly be cold.

"Come on, I don't even think I'll be that deep for you," Micheal said as he held out his hand for Willow to take and she slipped off the edge, feeling his arms go around her to pull her upright against the slight current the boat was sitting in.

"Guess I misjudged that," he said as he pulled her against him, as they walked up to the grass. Willow's eyes went to the three men that were standing under the shade. Amanda was nowhere to be seen. As they walked up closer she could hear their conversation.

"Just because I told you where they might be didn't mean 'Hey Vic, come on down!' They came out here for a reason." Eric said as Vic rolled his eyes at the shorter man.

"You had better remind your friend who he's talking to or he'll be out of a job in about 5 minutes," Vic said, his face turning towards Tommy and then Micheal.

"You better remind yourself who gave you your job first. Because you hardly are in the position of firing anyone," Micheal said, as he handed his sandals off to Willow, with a slight smile.

"How about you go inside with Amanda, we are just going to be a second," he said as Willow took his sandals in her hands and turned to walk back up to the house and saw the way the Vic was looking at her, with utter hatred. And she could feel his eyes following hers as she continued her ascent on the slight slope back up to the house. Setting his sandals next to the others and opening the sliding door and seeing Amanda peering through the shades down at the men, sipping on a new beer.

"Who needs reality tv when you have it right in front of you?" she joked until she saw the look on Willow's face and all humor was gone from her face.

"Sorry, I think this'll be my last beer for the day. Who is that?"

"Vic Andersen, Micheal's Agent. And Eric works under him with going out and basically doing his job for him," Willow explained, walking into the kitchen, leaving a trail of wet footprints across the carpet in her wake. Opening up the stocked fridge and grabbing for a beer as well. Walking back to kneel on the couch, elbows resting against the top of the couch, and looking out through the blinds at the three men on the beach.

"So if he's his agent and we are on vacation, then why is he here?" Amanda questioned, just as they saw them all scream.

Or at least that's what Willow could tell from the look on Micheal's face as he was being pushed away by Eric, as Tommy held back Vic as well. As Vic was waving a piece of paper in one hand and his phone in another.

"Crap, let's go," Willow said as they both set their beers on the windowsill and opened the sliding door and heard yelling down by the beach. Seeing Micheal in Vic's face as Vic was waving something in Micheal's face and then was pointing the direction of Willow as she ran down with Amanda to calm the situation down.

Nineteen

Willow and Amanda ran out of the house and out onto the beach. Seeing Vic in Micheal's face waving what looked like to be a document in Micheal's face. With Eric and Tommy trying to pull them apart.

"What is happening? Why are you even here? Didn't he tell you he was leaving?" Willow asked, exasperated at Vic. She had known something had happened between him and Micheal after their encounter after the movie premiere. She had known that from what she had seen from their body language. And to come all the way out here to start it up again.

"Can you tell your girl to not ask me questions, since she's part of the problem?" Vic asked, looking over Willow's head and over at Micheal. Making Willow's blood boil at the thought of him asking Micheal instead of talking to her directly. As Tommy pulled Vic away.

"If you wanna ask questions, you talk to me. Not about me. And what are you talking about? Part of the problem?" She asked, getting a glimpse of what Vic still had in his hand and saw that it wasn't just a piece of paper but a photo.

"This, this was sent to me with a message about sending this and the others to magazine publications everywhere," Vic said as he straightened it out. It was a photograph, a very close-up photograph of Willow and Vic in a very intimate embrace under the pier from their date before they went to the movie premiere.

"Wait, that's what this is about?" She said turning to Micheal and seeing the anger in his face.

"Yes, he got them in his email, or Eric did. He got pissed at him for overlooking the email. But he did exactly what he was supposed to. Send something critical like that to Vic. But he didn't check his damn email. But that's not the half of it. He wants to actually pay the person and release the photos, right Vic?" Micheal said. And all Willow could do was look over at Vic like how everyone else was looking at him.

"What? She is part of the problem. She's a distraction. Doesn't mean that this shouldn't be twisted into a good thing."

"A good thing? We left to get a break from the press after the movie premiere because I knew they would be at the bit, just waiting around to catch me out in Los Angeles. But they wouldn't be out here. Unless you are going to just oh I don't know get them out here too?"

"You don't get it. You haven't worked on a piece in a while and there's a show coming up. What better way of drumming up things for that? And yet you want to maul me for taking something that could be twisted negatively, like a distraction from your artwork to hangout with a girl, because that is what this is. A complete distraction. So I might as well take what is handed to me and twist it. You are involved with someone since no one has seen anything from you since you got out of the hospital. Yes, Eric has been covering your social media. But there is only so much past content of yours that he can reshare before people ask questions about new projects," Vic explained.

"I'm a distraction. Wow, ok," Willow said as she stepped

away, seeing the look of anger that was on Micheal's face at Vic disappear. And turn into worry.

"You aren't a distraction at all. This is a needed break. That we both need. Plus, I'm still needing to go to physical therapy despite someone else thinking that isn't required. I already have enough pieces that I've worked on for this that are going to be replicated for each location for people to buy," Micheal said looking over at Vic accusingly.

"Just because you want to push me to work doesn't mean that I'm even physically ready to be doing that. So stop pushing. And stop saying that Willow is a distraction, as if she's some type of negative force. When we both know I've been working more on projects since meeting her. As if the person who I love would bring a negative impact into my life," Micheal said, looking from Vic and back at Willow.

"You're not a distraction. We both needed this break," he said before turning to Vic.

"I don't want you to be doing anything like that without my permission. Eric isn't the one that should be worried about his job at all, it's you. Thinking you can take photos that other people took of moments of intimacy and release them out to the public. I wouldn't mind, of course. But I have an ex wife that would call me the second seething, because we all know she's jealous. And then using my son as an excuse. And I don't want that or need that frankly right now. You've wasted your time in coming here. Ask for that person's copies of everything though and pay them the amount they quoted that other publications would have paid him for them," Micheal said, as Willow's head was spinning at the news, as she started walking back up to the house since everything seemed to have been resolved between the two of them. Because Vic thought she was a negative distraction to Micheal's creative processes, which was a completely different tune that he had been singing before the photos.

That wasn't the only thing that made her feel uneasy. That word. He loved her. Or so he thought now. Until it would all turn in another direction. Like last time. Willow walked back up the house, hearing Vic's car starting up and leaving as she went to the fridge and grabbed over one beer and went into the master bedroom and closed the door behind her.

TWENTY

Willow walked into the master bedroom of the river house. Bottles of cold beer in her hands, placed them others on top of the dresser and flopped down on the bed. Puffing her hair out of her face as she ran through the events that just transpired between Micheal and his agent Vic Andersen. And it still didn't feel real.

"He said that he loved me. Of course he did," she said aloud, still confused at it. And also terrified. Because the last time someone said that, other than Amanda, was the person who thought he could control her. Put his hands on her. And Willow took the bottles of beer with her. Setting some on the dresser and grabbing one as she flopped down on the bed.

He really said that he loved her. When the last person who said those words was Andrew. Maybe meaning them at first, but then decided that it would be ok to put his hands on her. Demean her and make her feel like she couldn't do anything without him knowing about it.No, she wasn't about to let that happen again.

She popped open the beer, and threw the metal bottle cap

onto the floor. Hearing it contact the hardwood flooring. She took a sip of the beer, contemplating what she was going to do. As well as why Micheal would even say that out loud to anyone else in defense of her before actually saying that to her first.

"Hey, you ok in there?" Amanda said as she knocked onto the master bedroom door and tried the handle again, jiggling it and hearing nothing on the other end of the door. Not Willow throwing things or the television being on. Just silence.

"I know why you are freaking out, ok? I get it. Now let me in so I can talk you down from the ledge you have yourself over right now in your head over this," she said as she leaned against the door, and then looked up at Micheal.

"Told you, if I can't get in there. It's certainly not happening with you. Unless you have ways I'm not aware of," Amanda said as she stepped away from the door and gestured for him to take a try at talking to Willow. He knocked on the door and heard movement in the room.

"Hey, it's me. I want to talk. I know I should've told you that first. I didn't say it to get Vic off my back or yours to get him to leave. What I said was what I meant. I love you Willow," Micheal said as he stepped away and Amanda followed him as he walked down the stairs to the first floor.

"You realize that the whole point was for you to go in there and talk to her, right? If you don't, she's just going to spiral in her head about this,"

"Yes, I know. But I just remembered that I have copies of the keys for all the rooms hidden somewhere. Couple years back, Evan pulled the same thing, locking himself in one room. That was when Pam and I were going through a rough patch before divorcing and he thought locking the door with us inside the room and not letting us out until we talked it out would be helpful. After that I got copies of all the room keys so it wouldn't happen again," Micheal said as he started opening drawers in the kitchen, and rummaging through them until he came up with a set of keys.

"Well I'll give it to Evan, I don't think I would've thought of locking you two in a room, hell after seeing her in person I think I would've opened the back door to let you run away," Amanda joked, causing Micheal to laugh.

"That was the past, and we didn't work out. And see, I think I have enough experience to deal with this situation. After all, I have a teenage son. So I know how to talk people out of locking themselves in their rooms after something. Except I don't think I would've seen this coming because of me confessing my feelings for her," he admitted, walking back up the stairs to the master bedroom. And going through the keys to find the one that fit the master bedroom door. And putting it through the keyhole and turning it and the knob. Opening the door to Willow laying on the bed with a beer in hand and tears streaming down her face.

She was quick to wipe her face as she looked at Micheal and Amanda.

"I'm just going to let you two have a moment," Amanda said as she patted Micheal on the shoulder and walked back down to the first floor.

"I guess I can't lock myself away to drink in peace," Willow said with a slight laugh, more to herself and her situation than anything else.

"Well when someone runs away after I admit my feelings for said person to them, I have to come and check on them. Especially after grabbing the last of the beers from the fridge of herself," he said, nodding in the dresser's direction that had the other three beers sitting on them, collecting condensation on the glass bottles from having sat out for a couple minutes because of the Laughlin Nevada heat.

"I need a few minutes to myself to think here, ok. You realize the last person who said those words to me. Was the last person I thought I could trust, and he took that trust that I gave him and ruined it. And ruined me," she said, taking a sip of her beer.

"He didn't ruin you. He's a grade A asshole for taking your trust and using it against you for so long. And so help me if the cops find nothing soon I'll be going out there looking for him, along with Eric and Tommy, alright? Because just thinking about him, and what he did to you," Micheal said as he took one beer off the dresser, as Willow watched him, waiting for what he was going to do.

And he simply popped the top off the beer and chugged it, as Willow started laughing and Micheal did as well trying to cover his mouth.

"I thought you were going to hulk out and throw the beer bottle against the wall,"

"You think I would do that after just finishing renovations on this place myself? Hell no! Now I was thinking about opening the balcony door and just chucking the bottle outside but glass," he said, waving the bottle in his hand.

"Oh artistic and environmentally friendly, the two caveats that I didn't think I would find so sexy," Willow said, making Micheal smile.

"oh really?" he questioned as she nodded, taking a last sip of her beer and throwing it into the trash can.

"Yes, really. And frankly, I didn't want to admit this but seeing you go toe to toe with your manager earlier and defend me and Eric, was a kind of turn on," Willow said with a shrug of her shoulders as she watched Micheal down the beer that was in his hand and put it down on the dresser before getting on the bed with her.

"So what? Are they good? Bad?" Eric asked as Amanda walked down the stairs quietly, just as the sound of music started playing from the master bedroom.

"Oh, I think that means they are all good to go. She was in a spiral about him saying the big L word not to her in private, but with everyone else around. And apparently sex is what she needed to get her head on straight about it," she replied with a shrug of her shoulders.

"I can see where she is coming from, though, her past and hearing that in Vic saying she's a distraction to him. Hell, I'm waiting for that speech from him about you frankly," Eric said as Amanda tilted her head to the side and raised a brow at him.

"Oh really? I'm stopping you from what? What? re-sharing Micheal's art on his social media platform?"

"Hey it's more than that. I'm basically doing what Vic is supposed to be doing. There were WAY more photos than the one that he showed up with, very interesting ones. I just don't know how someone could've gotten so close without them noticing," Eric pondered as Amanda shrugged her shoulders.

"Shouldn't you be asking the camera boy over there?" Amanda said, nodding over toward Tommy, who had his head in the fridge, and popping back up and looking at both of them.

"What?"

"How would someone get that close without them noticing?" Eric said as he shifted his attention to Tommy.

"Different lenses. There are huge zoom lenses that someone can buy to stand far away from the subject to get crisp photos like that. Most of the time, those are used for wildlife photography. But I can see someone that is a paparazzo using something like that as well from a distance, but it's not that common."

"Says an actual member of the paparazzi peeps," Amanda said jokingly.

"Hey, have you ever taken photos of Micheal like that to actually spin around so Vic could sell them to the press?" she asked, just wondering if Vic would stoop so low as to do something like that.

"I haven't done that. And I never would. You know, I have a moral compass. I work for Micheal, not Vic. So he's never really been on to tell me what to do. I just come along to the events so I can take the photos that Eric will use to share across social media and then maybe share with other platforms for a price as well."

"Well that sounds a lot more exciting than working at a grocery store," Amanda said with an air of jealousy.

"Hey, everyone has elements of a job they do that they don't like. Ours just coincide together in our hatred for working near Vic," Eric commented as he wrapped his arm around Amanda's shoulders and squeezed her closer to him.

"Which, speaking of vicinity, why don't we go out, check out the town and get something to eat, since I think they are going to be awhile," Tommy said as he grabbed for the keys to the car.

"Ok, but I'm just wearing a bathing suit with a coverup. Don't you think I should change?" she asked, as she saw them both look her up and down slowly, as her face heated at having both their undivided attention.

"Maybe a t-shirt and shorts? Cause all we have to do is grab t-shirts and we are golden," Eric said, patting her shoulder, as they all went to change clothes and get out of the house.

Willow rolled off of Micheal and grabbed the remote for the speaker system, clicking it down a few notches. Waiting to hear some sorts of sounds around the house.

"oh, they definitely left," Micheal said as she turned to face him, seeing his hair in different directions.

"how do you know?"

"they aren't the type to just stay sitting around while we are having sex. Probably took Amanda out to explore the town around here."

"I don't know about you, but that actually sounds like fun. Even though we both kind of already explored around by ourselves this morning when we were out getting sandals for myself and breakfast for everyone else,"

"so, what you're saying is that she's possibly going to pretend like that didn't happen and act all intrigued and surprised with them?" he questioned, as he rolled onto his side to face her.

"wouldn't be the first time," Willow joked with a wiggle of her eyebrows as Micheal laughed at her joke.

"oh, that was a good one. Funny and slightly dirty. If I didn't know any better, I would think you spent more time around Eric."

"Amanda is like the female version of Eric. It's why they seem so perfect for each other," Willow said as she ran her fingers through her hair, getting up out of bed and feeling her head spin.

"remind me to not drink out of anger. It isn't good for me. I'm short so I don't have that much room to fall like others so I end up feeling the impact more," She said, grabbing some clothes and going into the bathroom, hearing Micheal chuckling at her joke the entire time she was in the bathroom changing.

"no, I don't think so. Drunk you is actually pretty funny,"

Willow opened the door as she was running a brush through her hair, poking her head out into the bedroom.

"well, see now we might have to get someone to drive us, because if I remember correctly you have been drinking,"

"drive us? Where would we possibly go? What if I just want a night to myself with my girlfriend?" He questioned, getting up and putting his boxers on and joining her in the bathroom. She could feel his fingers sweeping over the back of her neck, moving her hair from the back of her neck to the side as he placed a kiss on the exposed skin.

"So you want to just have dinner here? Just the two of us. No three musketeers joining in on the fun like last time?" she questioned him playfully, looking back and seeing him roll his eyes at her comment.

"never planned on them crashing the trip, so we have to work with the time that we are given. It's like trying to squeeze in some quiet time or do chores when a kid is asleep, you know?"

"Yes, I bet you know that feeling all too well. I, however, haven't. Closest thing that I have to that was studying around Amanda's work schedule when I still was in college. That was interesting, considering she would have night shifts and then want to make most of the days when I wasn't in class hanging out with me. Those were a lot of sleepless nights,"

"hey have that but still have that be around when you have a teenager. Can't wait until..." he said, trailing off as Willow looked at him through the mirror with her head tilted to the side, wondering what he was going to say.

"Can't wait until what?"

"nothing, nothing at all. Just get ready and I'll do the same. Then we can figure out what we want to make for dinner because you are helping me out," he said as he got out of the bathroom to let Willow finish brushing her hair out. Leaving her with questions about what he was going to say before he cut himself off.

Twenty-One

Willow was looking into the fridge and seeing what was left of the items they had bought the day before at the grocery store. With having three other people as part of a group, the food went exponentially quicker than had been intended.

"Hey this impromptu cooking dinner might have to turn into an impromptu going to the grocery store because everyone is here. Plus, drunk equals devouring food," Willow shouted out hoping Micheal would hear her.

"That's ok. That means we can probably get something out anyway," he said as he walked into the kitchen and peeked into the fridge to consider the amount of food that was in the fridge.

"Yeah, they do kind of end up eating a lot of food. We should definitely go to the grocery store," he said as he went to grab the SUV keys that were on the shelving that was close to the front door.

"Alright, but beware, I'm hungry. That means we are probably going to be getting more things than we needed," Willow warned as she walked right behind him out of the river house and into the SUV.

Putting the last of the bags into the bag of the SUV, Micheal closed up the backdoors as Willow was putting the cart into one of the cart corrals that were close by. Passing him his drink that she got him at the little coffee place that was inside the grocery store before they left it.

"Don't worry, it's decaf coffee. Just thought you would want something too," she said as she got into the passenger seat.

Micheal looked behind both of the front seats and back at the bags and bags of groceries.

"You think it would be ok if we went through a drive-thru and then back to the house to unload everything? Cause I am hungry,"

"Yes, that explains the odd things you put in the cart," she joked as she sipped on her drink.

"Hey, so were you, miss. I need a cake mix and 'I swear I'll make it tonight," he said, making his voice a higher pitch to mimic Willow's voice, as a fist came and punched him in the arm.

"Ouch! Hey!" Micheal exclaimed as he dramatically rubbed the arm that she had lightly tapped.

"Hey yourself. you better watch it or you'll be off the cake list for sure tonight, mister," Willow joked as he shook his head, starting the car

After putting the groceries away, Micheal and Willow sat outside on the back porch since it was so warm out.

"You know I wouldn't have really pegged you for fast food, but yes, you ate McDonald's after the premiere, so now I don't know what else could surprise me,"

"You mean other than knowing that there are photos of us floating out there from our date at the pier?" Micheal questioned, taking a measured sip of his beer.

"oh, we are on that again,"

"Yes, yes we are. I know it's not your fault but god, he just makes me so mad sometimes. I get that he's my manager but to just think that buying those photos off and spinning the story. Or even feeling like he needed to spin the fact that I am with you is crap. There have been other times he's tried to pull stuff, but this is a whole new one. I'm definitely having a talk with him when we get back."

"You know you don't have to defend me, right? If it hurts your career–"

"The thing is that it won't. you are far from a distraction. Hell, he even said before that you were my muse. He just said that because he's pissed, he actually has to do his job with this coming up instead of just sitting on his ass and getting paid to do it. Would rather give my money over to Eric and Tommy more for that kind of behavior than Vic," Micheal said quickly with a tone of conviction in his voice.

"See, but when you get down to it. If I didn't come into the picture, you wouldn't be in this situation right now. You wouldn't have to go to physical therapy for your hand because you got shot in your arm messing with your nerves in your hand," Willow said, her voice low, replaying what Vic said about her. And she felt like he was right. If she had not been around. If she had not picked that school to substitute at, her life and his would be very different right now. She downed her beer and slid out of her seat as Micheal looked over at her.

"what are you doing?"

"I'm going to pack. Vic is right, I am a distraction. I should have never–"

"don't, don't go down that train of thought. I thought I walked you away from that earlier. You think you are the only one having a hard time. Sweetheart, I left Los Angeles because I needed a break from Vic more than I did the paparazzi that were trying to report anything they could figure out about this," he said, gesturing between the two of them.

"Are you sure Vic doesn't have his hand in that too? Hell, what if he was the one that hired that photographer and just wanted to spin it on you to release the footage?" Willow questioned as she moved away from the table and stood up to her full height.

"I said nothing that said otherwise. He's my manager. He's not automatically safe in my thoughts of being involved with this. Getting my name out there and dealing with events is his job. He sees me being with you and wrapped up in this entire issue, probably as a good thing. And just wants to rile me up so we separate, don't fall into the trap that he's set," Micheal said, standing up and putting his hands on the table as he looked over it at Willow.

"Here's the thing. I've been having this nag at me all day. I can't help but compare you to Andrew. Right when you said those words. That was my immediate thought. That the last person who said that to me outside of Amanda that seemed to mean it was Andrew. And now my defenses are up because that's when everything changed when I was with him. And I don't want that to happen with us," she said, turning away from him and looking out into the pitch darkness of the water that wasn't too far from where she stood.

"You think I would do that to you? Hurt you? I waited for you, which I am glad that I did. It was worth it, sweetheart, but it was a hell of a wait that was hard for me."

"waiting to have sex with me until I felt like I could trust you? That was hard for you?" Willow questioned as she looked over her shoulder at him, her mouth turned down at the thought of that.

"that is not–" Micheal said as Willow threw her hand up to stop him from talking.

"no, no, you said what you said. Must've really had a set of blue balls on you after our time in my apartment when Amanda interrupted us, huh? Guess it's going to bother you when I tell you I want more space, because I need to think about this, us, and if there is something to it or not," Willow said, walking inside the house, leaving Micheal outside by himself.

TWENTY-TWO

Willow closed the door behind her. Leaving Micheal outside as the rushing of emotions hit her. That he thought that waiting for her was hard. To be ready to be with him. When he didn't realize that for her, it was so hard to wait out that much for herself to be with him. But she had known that she had to wait, to make sure he would not flip after getting what he wanted.

Little did she know that could have been a possibility even after waiting so long to have sex with him. She really didn't think he would do that now. Then again, things she never thought would happen did with Andrew. So her judgment wasn't exactly on par at all.

She walked up the stairs to the master bedroom and locked the door. Which reminded her he had the keys to all the rooms. So she went to her bag, grabbing a notebook and tearing out a page from it and scribbling a message of 'don't come in, I need some space' on the piece of paper. And then going into the kitchen to grab tape to stick it onto the master bedroom door.

And closing the door behind her. The exhaustion from the

fights all this afternoon hit her, as she climbed into bed feeling her eyes droop as she cuddled up to one pillow and felt into an unrestful sleep throughout the night.

Getting up the next morning, Willow rolled over, expecting Micheal to be there and to not have listened to the note that she left outside the door. But he wasn't there. She got up from the bed, shielding her eyes from the incoming morning light. Accompanying it was the heat as well. Which explained why she felt sweaty all over. And didn't have a restful night's sleep. Because she didn't turn on the air conditioning that was just for this room. Which she completely forgot about since she just went to bed, not even changing her clothes at all from what she had worn for the evening, which was shorts and a t-shirt.

She cleared her throat, feeling a tickle in her throat. Either from the fighting or because of the weather. She walked into the bathroom and looked at her reflection in the mirror and saw that she looked like absolute crap. Her hair was everywhere since she didn't put it in a ponytail before she went to sleep. Her eyes were red because of the endless amount of nightmares that plagued her throughout the night. Some were replays of the attack at Micheal's house from weeks prior. And others were just about the fight that happened between Vic and Micheal but ending with Micheal agreeing with Vic and making her and Amanda leave so he would no longer have distractions from his art.

Rubbing her fingers underneath her puffy eyes, she grabbed a notepad piece of paper, writing out the list of things. Which was already a long list of things. That she had been keeping track of since the trip to the Santa Monica Pier with Micheal. Things that she knew she needed to bring up in therapy. Which Willow didn't think would be helpful at first. She just went to placate

Micheal since it was his suggestion to go. But being there. On her own. And just getting to talk about everything. Let it out to a stranger that knew little about her? It felt wonderful getting all those pent-up feelings about the situation out. And not having to worry about constantly bothering Amanda about these things. Yes, she was Willow's friend, but she shouldn't have to carry that burden of having to hear everything that Willow was feeling.

Plus, Willow felt like she was a broken record of certain topics. Which she realized she would be until there was some type of resolution with things. And with everything that happened yesterday, that just added to the stress. At that, she got her bag and put it on the bed, and started grabbing some of her stray clothing items to put back into her bag. She didn't know for certain if she was leaving. But she just wanted to have everything ready in case she left.

Grabbing a comb from one of the bathroom drawers, she started brushing out her hair slowly. Giving her mind some time to calm down from the vast amount of things that were going through it at the moment.

There was knocking on the master bedroom door as she peeked her head out of the bathroom. She waited for another knock and then heard a softer voice than expected.

"hey, what happened? Can you let me in?" Amanda asked as Willow opened the door to let her friend in, who looked more than confused.

"What's up? I get up to make coffee and I see Micheal laying out across the couch,"

"We had a fight last night. He brought up Vic again. Somehow it got to us and waiting for sex and I said that it must've been hard for him to wait so long. And now we are here cause I asked for space to figure out for myself where we stand,"

"oh so you're imploding this then? I've been waiting for it,"

Amanda said as she sipped her coffee, as Willow snatched it from her friend's hand and sipped it, making a face as the sugary contents hit her tongue.

"how the hell do you drink this? This is a cavity maker for sure,"

"good thing I have a great dental plan. But seriously, I've been waiting for you to implode this. I was just thinking about how well you guys have been doing. Then the fight with Vic happened yesterday, and I had a feeling you would do this."

"What exactly? He said that it was hard for him to wait,"

"Well it was for you too, you told me before. So why are you vilifying him for the same feelings that you felt? You are just using an excuse you can to not be happy," Amanda said as she snatched her cup back from Willow.

"no, I'm not. I just want to think about us, and our situation. Since his manager things that I'm a negative force in his life,"

"Oh yeah, just THINKING about it, right," Amanda said, not convinced as she looked past Willow and saw her bag on the bed all packed up.

"what? I just put some clothes back into my bag."

"oh sure, that's what that is. Someone is trying to make their getaway more seamless for sure,"Amanda said, sipping at her coffee and looking back knowingly at her friend.

"this isn't that at all,"

"Girl, I've known you since community college. I know you better than anyone else in this house. I know when those wheels in your head turn to find an out. Which, ironically, was a thing before Andrew. Which I will never think would be a thing with Micheal. He's nice. We both know that. So you are comparing him to Andrew again because he went south after professing his feelings for you. Or you just want to have it implode before it gets anymore serious between the two of you," Amanda said with raised brows at her friend. Willow sighed, turning away from her friend and bracing herself on the bed.

"ok, this might be that. How am I supposed to react when he professes his feelings to me during a fight with Vic over these photos that got taken of us? Like he couldn't tell me that first when we were alone. Because then it looks like he's just saying it to get Vic off his back. Didn't work though, since I already know he's going to be on his ass about producing more pieces of art," Willow admitted, turning around and laying on the bed and looking back up at her friend.

"you have a minor point with how he went about it. Like no lie if those two did that to me, which they would never THINK of doing. I would hand their asses to them, of course. But to, like, implode this relationship over it?"

"it's not just that, it's the entire relationship being surrounded by drama,"

"Honey, you brought in at least half the drama with crazy Andrew. Which I'm not blaming you for at all. but Micheal is also a celebrity with his own drama that he brought in as well. And that combined is going to be crazy. It's as simple as that. And despite that, before all this professing his feelings, you seemed pretty down to being involved with him. Sounds more like you don't think that you deserve him," Amanda said with a tilt of her head, making Willow grit her teeth.

"ah, that's it isn't it? You don't think you deserve happiness after everything you've been through? Girl, he's a good thing for you despite all the drama. Hell, we wouldn't be here right now if you didn't think you deserved it a little," Amanda said, gesturing with her coffee cup to the master bedroom that they were currently sitting in.Willow just thought it over. There was a bit of truth to what Amanda was saying.

"Alright, I won't leave. I just need space for some time," Willow compromised, as Amanda smiled.

"good, cause I didn't want to leave this trip early,"

"wait? you were planning on leaving with me?" Willow said, surprise crossing her face.

"hell yeah, I was going to leave with you. That's what friends do. Stick-to-fucking-gether because I know you would do the same for me,"

"now get the fuck up off the bed so we can go hangout on the beach. Just us. We can brainstorm what we are going to do today while we sit out under the sun or the shade. Depends on how strong of sunscreen I have in my bag," Amanda said, pulling Willow up into a standing position and pushing her out of the master bedroom with Amanda right on her heels walking down the stairs.

"don't look at the couch, just go past or we can go out the front door and go find a bar somewhere,"

"Amanda, it's like 10am,"

"Willow, its Laughlin. We can easily go to one casino to get some drinks at one buffet. Right there. That's our plan!" Amanda said as she grabbed for the keys and pushed Willow toward the front door. She grabbed her phone and texted away on it, as Willow glanced down at Amanda's phone, only seeing.

"got it figured out. Have her with me leaving the house. Text me when you get done talking to Micheal," the text read, as Willow felt Amanda's hand on her back.

"Come on, let's go. Buffet food awaits,"

Twenty-Three

Willow sat across from Amanda's empty chair at one of the oldest hotel buffets. She had not been back since her time as a teen going out here during the summer. And nothing seemed to have changed at all since the years that had gone by. Still has the same buffet with the same array of food. Amanda was currently walking up back to the table with her plate piled high with an array of breakfast foods. Eggs, bacon, English muffin, toast, hash browns.

"you realize it's not like a one plate deal? You can go back for more once you are done eating what is on your plate."

"Hey, I like to have a lot on my plate at once. Gotta get the most out of what I'm paying for this," Amanda said, sitting down across from Willow as she started diving into her plate of food, as Willow just moved items around her plate, sipping at her coffee. Hoping that it would all help with the hangover she was experiencing at the moment. Trying to have deep conversations about relationships with a raging headache was not something she wanted to go through. So focusing on her plate of food and slowly picking at it was what she wanted to do.

"So you let Eric and Tommy know where we were. So they could tell Micheal where I was?" she questioned, wanting to ask about the text that she saw Amanda get on her phone.

"yeah I did. I think they were going to also take him out for breakfast. Get food in the both of you to go against the hangovers I know you both have from drinking last night," Amanda said as Willow looked over at her with wide eyes.

"Please, just cause we weren't there last night didn't mean we didn't see the evidence in the trash this morning of all the beer bottles in the trash can. And I know you are a lightweight, so eat up. I saw there were muffins, eat up," Amanda said, taking one item off her plate, a blueberry muffin, and slid it over to Willow. Who took it and started unfeeling the wrapper away from the pastry item and took a big bite out of it.

"drinking that much last night didn't help. Hell, all day it didn't help. I think I was just trying to distract myself from everything that happened yesterday."

"I don't blame you there. But at some point, you both are going to have to talk to each other about this."

"We already did. Last night. Remember? Didn't end well? Why did you bring me out here to avoid me leaving the entire trip way early? I've already scheduled out an appointment with my therapist when I go back because I'm going to need it. Already have a list of topics that have been rattling around in my head since I left that premiere that I wanted to talk out with her," Willow said to Amanda as Amanda nodded.

"Good, take some of that burden off of me," Amanda said as Willow tilted her head at her.

"You know I never intended for it to be like that at all," Willow said, feeling even worse about how much she vented to Amanda about everything. Realizing that Amanda never did the same to her, or at least not to the same extent.

"It's fine. Now you have a balance. And talking to someone

that can actually sort it out for you and try to work through it. Another thing in the pro-Micheal corner frankly," Amanda commented with a smile as she reached her hand across the table to Willow's and squeezed it affectionately, causing Willow to smile.

"Yeah, I guess. She is going to have a lot to work through. Or more like the both of us, really. Already have it scheduled for the day after I get back. Then I think I'll go to the district office to see who I can talk with about my job situation. If what Julie had said before about not hearing that, I won't be able to work because of the Andrew fiasco the last time I was on a school campus,"

"I can see maybe not working at Evan's school anymore, but the others? Plus, it's not your fault. It's Andrew's for bringing himself into your workplace and making a scene,"Amanda said, taking a sip of her water, quickly and setting it down harshly.

"hey, it's fine. I'm going to deal with it. You don't have to get all worked up–"

"I feel like I do, though. If they think to blackball you from substitute teaching when they don't really know you. And how awesome you are. That would be on them, and then I would be majorly pissed. Hell if it comes to that I'll work my schedule around to show up to every damn school board meeting to vouch for you and to get you back on until they are tired of seeing my face and hearing my voice," she said with a conviction that made tears well up in Willow's eyes at her friend's devotion to her.

"Oh don't start crying, it's too early for that. I'm going to have to get a drink for you," Amanda commented, making Willow's emotions flip and laugh.

"Fine, fine. I won't cry. But if you are going to do that, if it seems to be that way, of course I'm coming with you to every meeting," Willow said, picking up her glass of water for Amanda to clink hers against.

"to being annoying assholes to the district if we have to!" Amanda said as they clinked their glasses together, laughing.

"Now come on, no more distractions. I want to eat this plate and go get another one. I want to at least try almost everything they have here," Amanda said, turning her attention to her overflowing plate and eating some items that were on it.

"Yeah, they have a good buffet. I told you as much when we drove here. And you wanted to go to another casino. Therefore, you trust my word. I'm never wrong with food recommendations,"

"Neither am I. That's why we are perfect for each other, as friends," Amanda added at the end, a smile creeping up on her face as Willow laughed at that.

"Oh yes, of course."

Willow wiped her face with a napkin and looked across the table at Amanda, who was eating the last bite on her plate.

"I really can't believe you did it. You ate almost everything that was laid out at the buffet," she said, shaking her head at her friend's gluttony.

"what? I'm just trying to get my money's worth out of it. Plus, sometimes I take these things as a personal challenge sometimes," Amanda said with a shrug of her shoulders as she got her purse from her chair behind her and put the strap over her shoulder.

"Are you ready to go?" she asked Willow.

"really? don't need a second to breathe? You ate everything,"

"You make it sound like I was trying to be like it was an

eating contest. I ate bites of everything, not entire pieces of everything, get it right," Amanda said as she got up, swaying a bit as Willow got up and pushed her friend back into her chair.

"Told you, you need a second,"

"Usually when I stand it helps. Guess not this time," she said as she slumped against the chair with a sigh. Willow shook her head at her friend and got up.

"what are you doing?"

"getting something else, because I paced myself, unlike someone," Willow said with a smile at her friend as she walked back towards the buffet. Grabbing a plate from one stack, and walking around the different arrangements of food. Stopping at a station that had an attendant where it was a make your own crepe station that they would make the crepe once the person selected the things they wanted inside the French breakfast item.

Willow looked at the items, debating between sweet or savory. Taking her time perusing the items, knowing that she was giving her friend's stomach more time to settle because of the mass amount of food she ate.

"what will it be?" the man said that was over on the other side of the counter, as she looked up at him.

"I'm debating between getting fruit or something savory," she pondered.

"Why not get both?" She heard as she looked next to her flinching, expecting Andrew to be standing there right next to her. Her hand clutching her chest as she heard a muffled voice until she turned to the attendant that was looking at her concernedly.

"miss? Are you alright? I was just saying that you could get one of each problem solved," he said as Willow nodded as she quietly pointed at the items that she would want in both of them. Trying to keep her thoughts from spiraling and wanting to run. Just like she did not that long ago when she was at the grocery store with Amanda that first night out of the hospital.

She knew that this was definitely going to be added to the list when she gets back to the river house later. The list she had started about things she wanted to talk through with her therapist.

Twenty-Four

After a bit of sitting down for a bit at the breakfast buffet to let Amanda's stomach settle, despite her protests, she and Willow did a bit of gambling before they got back into their car. On their way back to the river house. Willow was sitting in the passenger seat, looking out the window, feeling the warm sunlight coming in through the glass, heating her skin.

She turned the air conditioning on in the car as Amanda's eyes flicked towards her and then to her phone. Making Willow realize that throughout the morning, after they had left, her eyes were always on her phone. Because instead of putting it in her purse or in her pocket, like Willow had done, she instead had placed it face up on the table.

"you got something you are waiting for? Something about work? Because your eyes have been checking that screen all morning"

"not really. Just texted the guys after we had left if they needed us to run any errands before coming back. That's all," Amanda answered smoothly, as Willow shrugged her shoulders.

"We could always stop at a grocery store? I know we could

probably use more food," Willow said as Amanda turned on her turn signal, waiting to turn down a street.

"ok, you want to text them? Ask either of them what they would want?" Amanda said as she tapped at her phone, unlocking it and handing it to Willow.

Willow looked at Amanda's phone and saw that there was an open group chat thread Amanda was a part of along with Eric and Tommy. Willow texted the message about the grocery store and saw that there had in fact been another text earlier about errands. Willow scrolled back, trying to find that one text message about distracting her for a bit. But she didn't see that one. Making her think she had been just seeing things or this, in fact, wasn't the same message thread she had seen the text coming from. And she didn't know which one of them would have sent that text message either since she didn't know either of the men and Amanda would as of this moment.

"did you text them? what did they say?" Amanda said as Willow saw that Amanda's attention was split between the road and listening to Willow's response.

"yeah I did text them. They haven't–" Willow started to say, just as Amanda's phone dinged twice seeing text messages from Tommy and Eric came through.

"oh they just texted. Beer, water, and snacks? And then Eric just says EVERYTHING in all caps," Willow said with a slight laugh as she clicked off her friend's phone and put it back in the cupholder.

"oh of course he would say that. I can tell who checked the fridge and who's just hungry," Amanda replied with a laugh as she grabbed her phone quickly, opening it up and tapping away as her eyes flicked between the phone and the road as they stopped at a red light.

"What are you texting back?" Willow asked, curious since

her mind was still thinking about that mysterious text that Amanda got earlier.

"Oh nothing, just telling them we had a nice breakfast, and they missed out," Amanda said with a shrug of her shoulders and a smile. But Willow noticed the smile didn't quite seem right. She was definitely lying.

Willow was about to bring up the text as Amanda put her phone back in the cup holder and turned into the grocery store parking lot. Putting the car in park and pulling the keys from the ignition.

"beer, water, probably ice and fruit too? What do you think? Because I think fruit is going to be required since it's so freaking hot out," Amanda asked as they both got out of the car. Willow felt the heat hit her face first, just like a blast in the face from a dryer on high. Making her immediately put her hair up into a bun to keep her cool.

"That sounds nice. What about Jello? we can make jello shots?" she offered as they started walking into the grocery store.

"Oh yes, vodka in the heat," Amanda mused sarcastically, grabbing a cart once they entered the store making their rounds.

"You say that now, as if you wouldn't have an entire tray yourself?" Willow questioned playfully as Amanda hit her friend lightly on the shoulder.

"The men shall have their beers while the girls get the jello shots," Amanda agreed with a nod, turning the cart into an aisle, as she pulled Willow right behind her.

Amanda and Willow, each with a bag in hand, walked up to the entrance of the river house, finding the front door was already opening as they approached.

"there's ice in the back if you guys want to grab it. And cases of beer," Amanda said as she walked past Eric and Tommy. Eric sarcastically saluted her as Tommy rolled his eyes at his friend's reaction.

"Come on, let's help them out. That way we can get this stuff on ice quicker," Tommy said, walking past Willow as she walked inside, dropping the bags onto the counter.

"Where's Micheal at?" Willow asked as she looked around and didn't see him in the living room, or beyond out by the water from the angle where she was standing at the kitchen island.

"checking the lines on the boat, or that was what he did after you left. Wanted to make sure they didn't get loose overnight," Tommy said as he walked past them with two of the ice bags out of the back where the big ice chest was and the smaller one that they took with them on the boat.

Willow was turning her attention to getting the items out of her bags, as she glanced at Amanda, and saw that her friend was practically hanging onto the open fridge door. Her attention was completely gone from putting items that Willow was putting out onto the counter into the fridge. Instead her friend, as Willow saw by following Amanda's line of sight, eyes glued to watch Tommy taking the bags of ice and smacking them hard onto the concrete ground to break them up before putting them into the ice chest.

"Earth to Amanda? Hello Amanda?" Willow said, snapping her fingers, causing Amanda to blink and look over at Willow with a surprised look across her face. And Willow could spot the telltale signs of a blush starting up on Amanda's darker complexion.

"Sorry, blame mr. 'I-have-to-break-ice-shirtless' over there. It's not my fault the man has a great back. And ass," Amanda added with a smirk at Willow as they broke out in laughter as they continued on with their task of putting all the groceries in the fridge.

"ok, I think that is the last thing," Willow said, taking the plastic bags in her hands and throwing them in the trash.

"Now, comes the fun part, Jello shot making time," Amanda said as she untwisted the top of the bottle of vodka they also bought at the grocery store.

"Did I hear something about Jello shooters?" Eric said as Willow jumped, not noticing that Eric was walking in from the back with Tommy.

"Yeah, don't look at me accusingly. It was Willow's idea,'" Amanda said, putting her hands up at both of them. Causing Willow to look between her friend and the two men as their judgy looks went from Amanda to Willow.

"what? wait, have you actually experienced vodka drunk Amanda already?" Willow questioned with a smile at Amanda, watching her friend's eyes dart from her to Eric and Tommy.

"Yes, and it didn't end well," Tommy said with his arms crossed over his chest.

"Yeah, maybe Jello shooters aren't such a good idea," Eric said as he grabbed for the bottle of vodka, as Willow saw Amanda pout. And that was the first time Willow saw her friend not put up a fight over something. Which was not what Willow was expecting. Until she saw a smile creep up on Amanda's face.

"how about we still make the jello shooters and instead of going on the boat, you two stay with me? Supervise vodka-drunk-me while Micheal and Willow go off on the boat by themselves?" Amanda asked as she looked around the room, just as the sliding glass door opened and Micheal walked in.

Willow's eyes immediately went to him. And she saw his eyes scan the room, as if he knew he walked into the middle of a discussion. But his warm brown eyes landed on Willow and a look of sympathy crossed his face.

"What is this about you not going on the boat?" Micheal asked, as he walked further in the room, already wearing a t-shirt and swim trunks, as were Eric and Tommy.

"oh, they don't want me to go on the boat if I make jello shooters because of how I acted the last time I got drunk on vodka. So I made a compromise. I still make them and have a couple. They stay with me to supervise and you guys both go on the boat for a bit," Amanda said with a wink. That just made Willow narrow her eyes at her friend, waiting for some type of argument starting between her, Eric, and Tommy.

And after a second, they both nodded, as they both shared knowing looks between all three of each other. Which meant that something was up.

Suddenly Amanda was around the kitchen island and pushing Willow into walking toward the sliding glass door.

"what are you doing?"

"What does it look like I'm doing? jumpstarting the situation. Go off. Go have fun with Micheal," Amanda said behind her friend as she walked behind Willow to the already opened door, and then looked back at Micheal.

"Come on, let's go," she said, pulling Micheal out of the house to stand outside the sliding glass door as Willow looked on, shocked at her friend. As Amanda shut the glass door and waved at them.

"go on. Go reconcile out on the boat. Talk it out," Amanda said as Eric and Tommy joined her where she stood. Micheal simply shrugged his shoulders and started walking towards the boat.

Willow looked through the window at her friend as Amanda smiled and locked the lock of the door and waved at her again.

"go reconcile, you guys need time without us to work through stuff,"

Willow turned around and started walking quickly to catch

up to Micheal who was getting closer to the boat, as he walked out from the sand and onto the little dock that they tied the boat up to the previous afternoon.

"What happened to you having keys for everything? Can't you go unlock it?" she questioned. Micheal simply looked up from where he was kneeling next to the boat.

"If you are going to talk to me, please help to undo these ties while I start up the boat. And help me push off the boat from the dock," Micheal responded, avoiding Willow's question.

"Fine, but I'm going to be drinking the entire time. How long do you think we are going to have to be out there? Fifteen, twenty minutes? Until we can come back?" She questioned as Micheal simply held out his hand for her to take to steady herself when she got into the passenger seat of the boat.

"Just help me untie the ties," he said as he got in the boat and turned the key into the ignition to start the boat as they both went around untie the ropes that were on tied to the metal tie off spots on the boat. Taking up cushions from the seats and putting the ropes underneath them in the hidden compartments.

"Ok only the two buoys are left on the side," Willow said as she tied one and pushed off the front part of the boat and threw it onto the floor of the boat and sprinted to the back to remove the last buoy. Pushing off the boat out into the current of the river.

She was pushing up the cushions, and putting them in the backseat, catching Micheal smiling at her as he was putting sunglasses over his eyes.

"Despite you being in a poor mood because of all this, we make a great team. You can't deny that," he said as he clicked the ignition in as he turned the boat around to go upriver.

Willow sat down in the passenger seat and clicked open the radio cover and turned it on, clicking through the stations that it was picking up to listen to music. Turning up the dial so they could hear it over the sound of the boat's engine roaring.

She stopped at a station that was playing rock music. So she clicked the radio cover into place and pulled up the ice chest that was in the boat. Seeing that it was full to the brim with ice and a couple of snacks on top of the ice.

She took them out and then put her hand into the ice, fishing around for anything that her hand touched. Her hand came into contact with something as she pulled her hand through the ice chest with a can of cool beer and her hand dripped wet from the moisture. And cracking it open and taking a long sip before putting it in the cupholder.

"Do you want anything to drink? I can rummage around for water," she said, glancing over at him as he focused on the path in front of him as he was driving the boat.

"I'm fine for now. Looks like they even packed sunscreen too. Going to stop unless you want to turn red like a tomato," Micheal replied, shaking a can of aerosol that he got from the cupholder that was closest to him.

"Oh, they thought of everything then, didn't they?" she said as she raised a brow at him. As he looked at her with a look of confusion.

"What do you mean?"

"oh I thought I had been seeing things earlier, a text off of her phone. They definitely planned this," she said, her thoughts going to the extent at which they did this.

There was suddenly a sound coming from the boat motor, making Micheal looking toward the gauges and frowning at them as he tapped at two of them specifically.

"what's up?"

"the gas. I checked it yesterday when we got off the boat and both tanks were fine. So I didn't think that it would be a problem. But apparently it was. Unless this was a part of their plan,"

Micheal said as he clicked a button on the boat and the back of the boat where the engine cover was. Willow got into the driver's seat to take hold of the wheel to keep the boat straight and looked over at the levels. Sure enough, both gas tank levels were bone dry empty.

"So, what are we going to do? Float all the way back? How are we supposed to get back to the dock?" She asked, looking back at where Micheal was at, his head in the engine compartment where the engine was located looking around.

"Well see, I was going to check the gas tank levels myself first to make sure the gauges are broken or anything. Then if they aren't broken, I say we can go into slight panic mode but not yet," he said, turning back to look at Willow for a second, giving her a reassuring smile as he grabbed for a stick and then opened up the gas tank on one side and put the stick in. Willow didn't have to look back to hear the clunk that the stick made as it hit the bottom of the tank before Micheal brought it back up. And it wasn't wet at all. Completely free of any moisture that would have come from the tank if there had been gas in it.

She wasn't trying to panic just yet, as Micheal closed off that tank and went the two steps it took as he leaned over the boat to get to the other one, opening it up. As Willow crossed her fingers, hoping that the gas gauges were just broken.

And yet again after a minute, and Micheal retrieving the stick, it was dry again. He closed off the tank and then put the stick back in the corner of the engine compartment. And then turned and walked over to where Willow was sitting in the driver's seat, concentrating on keeping the boat away from the rocky bottom of the river and the ledges.

He clicked the bottom for the engine compartment to close again and then sat in the passenger seat, grabbing for the ice chest and popping the lid off. His hands rifling through the ice and grabbing a bottle of water.

"You want me to take over?" He asked as he took the top off and drank a sip of the water. And damn it if Willow didn't watch him through her sunglasses. Because she was still angry with him, not blind.

"No, I'm fine. I just want to know what we are going to do about this situation," she said as she fanned herself because of the heat.

"You have your phone with you? Maybe we can get a signal and call them back at the house? See if we can meet up and they can give us gas?" He offered, as Willow checked her pockets. Thankfully, in Amanda's haste to get her out of the house, Willow didn't dress for being out in the water, wearing her t-shirt and denim shorts from the morning. Her hand came into contact with her phone as she grabbed it and clicked it on. Immediately going to her contacts and dialing Amanda's number.

And listening to it ring. And ring.

"Come on, answer the damn phone, please!" And after a couple more rings,

"Hello? You already worked it out?"

Willow gritted her teeth and then responded in a sickly sweet tone, "yes, of course, we realized how stupid we were being after only a couple minutes out on the boat. No, not at all actually. We ran out of gas and we need you guys to meet up at some point. We can try to beach it close to another house or something and you can come with gas?"

All Willow could hear on the other end was Amanda pulling the phone away and repeating what Willow had just said as there was the sound of laughing on the other end.

"I knew it! I knew there was something weird about today. They must've siphoned the gas out last night or something,"

Willow said to Micheal as she put the phone back to her ear and hearing another voice on the other end of the call.

"So here's the deal. We syphoned the gas to give you both time to work out your stupid childish crap without us being around. I'll come with gas when you've figured it out," Eric said in a serious tone that she had only gotten a snippet of, but he sounded like he was serious. Micheal gestured for the phone from Willow as she passed it to him.

"Ok, we have figured it out. And we are on better terms than yesterday. We both realized that we were just being childish. So now can you come with the gas?" Micheal said, ending the call as Willow smiled. Good, he was also willing to lie to get them here to get the gas so they wouldn't be stuck out in the heat for too long.

"Well, we might as well drink to pass the time. Or well you can. Since I still need to drive this back," Micheal said as he passed another can of beer as Willow just finished the one in her hand and crushed it out of frustration and put it in the ice chest and closed the lid. Leaning back against the seat. Glimpsing out of the corner of her eye, Micheal's eyes going over her form.

<hr>

In no time, Willow had finished another beer, and she usually never drank like this. But her gaze went to Micheal more and more. Every time that she glanced at him and he caught her eye, she turned away, looking out at the river in front of him.

She was now sitting in the passenger seat since he said that it would be better if he sat in the driver's seat since she was the one that was going to be stress drinking for the both of them. And as every minute that passed, her mind was going south for thoughts about him.

She glanced over at him as he sipped at his water. His expression was unreadable because of the sunglasses that were covering his eyes as he corrected the boat.

Screw this.

"Put the flag up, I'm going in the water, I'm too hot," Willow said as she whipped her sunglasses off and took her phone out of her pocket and put it in the cupholder. Walking the few steps towards the back of the boat and jumping off the back into the cool water.

Coming up a second later and swimming to where the ladder was. Looking up and seeing that Micheal was looking back. One hand held onto the flag that showed that there was someone in the water, while his other was on the steering wheel.

She climbed back up. Feeling her t-shirt sticking to her like a second skin. Along with her denim shorts that didn't feel that comfortable when they were soaking wet. But she felt better than she did before she jumped in the water. With a glance down, she saw that her t-shirt was, in fact, sticking to her chest and to her bra, making it more visible underneath her light pink t-shirt.

She could feel his eyes working their way up and down her body, as she went to wring her hair out of the water as she sat back down in the passenger seat.

"Make sure you right the boat if it goes sideways. You made it look so good. Plus, it's hot as hell," he said as he passed her and dove from the back of the boat. Complete the opposite of how she went in, cautious. He drove in, gracefully surfacing as Willow leaned over the side.

"I'm sorry,"

"What?" He asked as he shook his head off the water as he gripped the ladder.

"I'm sorry. For comparing you to Andrew. It's because after he told me he loved me, that's when the relationship went south. And my brain, I guess, went into survival mode. Completely on the defense because I want this relationship. But after what happened, I can't help but think about how the previous one ended. I shouldn't have freaked out on your like that. You didn't deserve it," she said as Micheal came back up on the ladder and walked the couple steps back to the driver's seat, and sat opposite her in the passenger seat. She moved to face him, both their knees touching in the small walking space between the two seats.

"Trust me, I wouldn't say it if I didn't mean it. I've known that I've loved you for a while now. I just felt like I could express it to you now. I just wanted to take things slow. For both of us." He said as he took hold of one of her hands and continued.

"I'm not one to wait for sex, but I waited, and it really was worth it. And I know I shouldn't have complained about that to you, as if that was such a big deal. Because the other night made it so worth the wait for Willow. I love you," he said as he caressed her face lightly.

Willow moved to sit on his lap automatically at his confession, kissing him as he laughed at the unexpected move. Feeling his hands move down her back as she deepened the kiss. Just as they both heard an engine approaching them. They both turned and saw Eric coming up to them on a jet ski and a gallon of gas tucked against his foot.

"Guess my plan worked after all," he said as Willow hopped off Micheal's lap, feeling her face and chest heat at being caught making out by one of Micheal's friends.

"Hey, it's better that you came now with that then later," Micheal said with a wink towards Willow before he got up to retrieve the gas tank from Eric and started putting the gas in one of the tanks.

"Do you need anything? We have water if you want some," Willow offered as Eric waved the offer off.

"I'm good. Just wanted to take this out of you guys because I didn't want to hear more of Amanda pressing me about doing it or else she was going to... withhold things," Eric said slowly, making Willow laugh.

"Of course she would say that,"

"Ok, well, looks like we are good to go. I'll keep the gas container in the back. You are good to go," Micheal said as he turned the key for the boat and watched as the level of the gas gauge on one tank went up.

"Alright. See you back at the house. Hopefully, you guys won't doddle too long because we have something we want to talk about when you get back," Eric said, looking at Micheal pointedly with a smile as Willow noticed a twinge of a smile coming from Micheal. Making her realize he knew what his friend was talking about as he left them by themselves. Once again.

"I'm guessing you know what he's eluding too, then?" She questioned.

"Kind of. It was something they both mentioned to me last night to think about. We could go back now if you are so curious or..." he trailed off with a knowing smirk.

"Or we can go somewhere and start where we left off before Eric so rudely interrupted us," Willow suggested with a smile, as Micheal turned the boat around.

"I know just the place," he said as he went upriver, the opposite direction of the river house, as Willow felt her heart pumping faster as the boat sped up along the water.

Twenty-Five

Micheal drove the boat further upriver, making Willow question if they were both on the same page about what they were doing exactly. Staying out later despite getting gas in the boat.

"Micheal what are we doing exactly?" She asked, looking from the front of the boat and glancing at him.

"Trying to find a spot. There are beaches everywhere. Just have to find one that is secluded enough," he said, with an almost calmness in his voice. But his hands, one on the steering wheel and the other on the boat throttle. Both hands gripping both so hard that his knuckles here white. A dead giveaway that he was having a hard time waiting, just like Willow was.

After putting out an anchoring off the front of the boat to the beach, as well as the back. Willow felt her heart race as she watched as Micheal was rooting around in the back of the boat.

"What are you doing? It's anchored off? Unless you were

planning on not putting the moves on me after all?" She questioned playfully just as Micheal jumped out of the boat, two fluffy towels in hand.

"Oh, there's no question about that. I just remembered that I always have towels stashed in the boat in case I forget them," he said, wiggling his eyebrows at Willow suggestively. Shifting the towels under one arm and taking ahold of her hand and walking further away from the boat and deeper into the beach.

"Don't tell me this is where you bring all your hookups?"

"You know that you're the only one that I've been with since the divorce," he replied, flicking out his finger at Willow's nose playfully.

"This is a place we've gone to before me and the guys. It's more than the other beaches and it goes back aways. Giving us more privacy."

"See if the three stooges weren't at the house we wouldn't have to do this for privacy," Willow said, laughing as Micheal spun her around, his arms coming around her waist. And then his lips were on her, stopping her from laughing.

He let go of her momentarily to throw the towels down onto the hot sand, as Willow's hands clenched at her sides. Only for a second. She wanted to touch him, but went to her shorts, working at the button of her denim shorts. Slipping them off quickly, kicking them out to the side. Then taking off her t-shirt. Leaving her in only her bra and underwear. Looking up and seeing Micheal taking off his t-shirt and discarding it on the ground. Along with his sunglasses. His arms wrapped around her as he whispered.

"only have one condom with me, so we better make this worth it," he said, his face against her neck, making her laugh as he leaned back as he held her against him. "I'm sorry, but I think I'm going to have to get an explanation for why you would think you would have to have condoms in your swim trunks,"

"What's the Boy Scout saying? Always be prepared? Plus, with our fight yesterday, I had a feeling makeup sex would be in order today," he explained as he said right before he leaned back effectively, taking them both down in a fit of laughter that quickly changed into moans.

Laying out on the beach, Willow gasped in breaths or tried to as she felt her heart race. She glanced over and all she could see was Micheal's chest rising and falling just as rapidly and his eyes were closed, as if he was sleeping. Or trying to. After the disaster of the previous day, this is exactly where Willow wanted to be, needed to be. Away from everyone else and just with Micheal out in the sun.

She didn't want to leave, but also didn't want her phone to ring or for Eric or Tommy to come looking for them since it had been awhile since he came to give them gas in the boat.

"Micheal, we need to get going," she said as she turned to shake him.

"Go out on tour with me" he blurted out as he opened his eyes, surprising the hell out of Willow, who just looked down at him, trying to process what he just said.

"Go out on tour with you? Your art exhibition tour?"

"Yeah, that's what they were hounding me about and what Eric was alluding to before he took off back to the house," he explained as he sat up.

"I would love to go,"

"I'm sensing that there's a but coming right after that statement,"

"Well, I mean, I have a lot of stuff to figure out. I can't just go off with you. I have therapy that I am probably really going to need coming back from this trip to vent. Then there's the whole matter of my employment with the district hanging in the balance from what Julie told me when I was at the hospital. I need to go to the district office and talk to them and see what is up with that," Willow said, as her previous thoughts of bliss and contentment were now racing at the thoughts of all the things that she kept on hold with her life since the attack.

"You want me to go with you? Because—"

"No, I need to do this on my own," she said, running her hand through her hair, which she stopped once she realized she was doing the same thing that Micheal does when he's stressed. Living with him for a short time and she already was picking up his nervous habits. She got up, buttoning up her shorts, and fixing her messy hair back into a ponytail.

"I get that you have stuff going on. It's just an offer. Just think it over. I'm not asking you to completely take off the entire time with me. I think there are dates for around Los Angeles or adjacent at least so you don't have to travel," he said, and Willow could tell from his voice that he was hurt that she came up with what sounded like excuses to avoid going out with him.

"It's not that I wouldn't want to go. I want to see it. I have seen none completed pieces or even seen a show. Even if it was from outside the building years ago. I just have a lot going on that was put on pause when everything happened. If there are Los Angeles dates, count me in. Because I know those are at night. Which means you could probably stay at the house then, right?" She said, trying to rectify the slippery slope she realized she had sent herself on.

"Alright, I can go with that for sure," he said as she looked down and saw that a smile was on his face at her willingness to compromise. Then his arm was around her hips, the next second pulling her back down.

"I don't think I said we were done, unless I'm missing something," he said as Willow landed on top of him, making her laugh at the sudden movement that took her by surprise.

"Oh, really?" She questioned, as she moved off of him and noticed that he moved his hands to behind his head.

"Yeah, how about we just lay out for a minute? We'll still have enough of the day to go back whenever we want to. Leave them waiting in anticipation," he said with a wink.

"God, you are seriously the worst, you know that?" She asked rhetorically as she laid down next to him on the towel, soaking in the heat from the sun.

TWENTY-SIX

Willow looked at the piece of paper in her hand and then back at the big building and the numbers on the side of it.

"Guess this is it. I wonder how long it's going to take me to find the office though," she said aloud, as she got out of her car, and slung her crossbody bag, hand going to the side of it. Feeling a sense of calm, knowing that her gun was in her bag.

Since coming back from the hospital, she had been in the habit of keeping her gun with the safety on near her at all times.

Because you never know.

Willow walked up the steps wondering why Eric asked her to come here, unless Micheal was in the office as well. The only thing that she could think of was going through the final schedule for the gallery tour and letting her see the dates and locations.Walking up the steps, she bumped into someone.

"Sorry, excuse me,"

"No, excuse me," the male voice said, as she could hear the smile in it. And stopped where she was and looked to her left, her hands moving to her bag immediately.

Andrew was looking back at her. She knew that. He looked different. Different coloring of hair and it was longer. Facial hair now covered his face. But the eyes, his eyes they would never change.

"What are you doing here?"

"Oh, just making a visit, of course, dropping off some things," he said, tapping at the camera that was at his hip.

"You, you were the one that took those photos of us on the pier,"

"Ah, I knew you were the brains behind the little duo, that you would connect it fast," Andrew said, narrowing his eyes at her.

"Why? Why did you do it? Why did you attack me? Why did you kill Carmen? All because you couldn't get it through your head that it would not work?" She asked, knowing that there was a slim likelihood she never would get any answers to these questions at all.

"Because, Willow, it's quite simple, really. We never ended things at all. You simply walked away. And I just can't accept that. We should try again. After all, with all the media coverage over your relationship now, and maybe some things coming out, I think you would reconsider. Anyhow, I'll be seeing you on tour," he said, stepping away and picking up the camera and clicking it at her, as she stepped back from the flash as he chuckled to himself. With Willow staying where she was and just watching him descend the stairs.

And Andrew turned to look at her.

"Also, what are you talking about? Carmen? Dead? I would never, just remember I'll be watching" he said as a sinister smile appeared on his face while holding the camera in one hand, as he set it down to hang from his neck by the camera. Turning away and whistling happily as he walked down the street. Leaving Willow alone on the stairs. Holding onto the piece of paper that was shaking in her hands. Watching him until he was out of sight.

Before she turned and ran up the steps and into the building, her eyes were burning because of the tears that were threatening to fall from her eyes. But she was too angry to cry. No, she was in a screaming mood. And she knew exactly who she was going to confront next.

"I don't understand. I come to you and tell you about something. That I know Micheal has told you about. And you don't seem very empathetic at all," Willow said as she crossed her arms over her chest.

"Well, you see, I know about it. Micheal explained it further to me after Eric explained it to me. What you both went through was traumatic. But see, I was empathetic before I got a fist to the face out in Laughlin because of your antics with Micheal. I see it as a win-win now. I got someone that can help more with IT things and you are out of the picture," Vic said as he moved his left leg over his right knee, leaning back into his chair looking at Willow from across his desk.Willow narrowed her eyes at his admission.

"I can't believe you would do that. I don't mean me. I don't care if I don't see you. You're a straight asshole. But, doing this to Micheal, Vic? I'm sure he doesn't know about it yet. You've probably talked around it. Made sure that he never sees him. But once he finds out, you realize he's going to leave you. He will not have an agent that willingly hired someone that tried to kill him."

"I know, and that I know you. You'll run to him after this and tell him. That is unless your silence can be bought. I remember something about Micheal telling me about you wanting to go back to school, and that you'll be having to juggle substituting while getting your Master's Degree. That is, unless your tuition is paid for in full for the entire time and maybe some rent money for a place for you to stay at with that friend of yours. What was her name? Amanda?" Vic said as he smiled at her.

"You can't buy my silence. I care about him. It was enough that I had to see Andrew's face again. But I don't want Micheal to see it ever unless it's when he's behind bars," Willow said as she turned on her heel, walking out of his ornate office. Through the hallway and out the double doors. Stopping outside to catch her breath, as she leaned against the wall, feeling the tears streaming down her face, as she looked down at her hands that were shaking.

"God, I knew I should've visited my therapist before dealing with any of this at all," she said, wiping the tears from her face and walking down the steps. Without even gaining the information that she wanted to learn, which was the tour dates.

But she learned so much more than that today, things she didn't think she ever would have thought to have learned. Andrew has been around them for a while working for Vic. And Vic was the guy that Willow had presumed that he was. A lying snake.

TWENTY-SEVEN

Willow walked away from the building, her thoughts spiraling to seeing Andrew again. Being furious at seeing him, but also because she did nothing but stand there. And freeze. Which she never thought would happen after the last time she saw his face. After what he did to her and Micheal.

Add that to the list of things that she would have to talk to her therapist since she's the only one that she felt like she could voice her thoughts about everything. She could talk to Micheal but with how rocky everything seemed with the two of them since the river trip happened, she felt like she couldn't talk to him about what happened. Especially because she didn't want to trigger him over his own experience of the attack.

As well as Andrew's response. He said that he didn't kill Carmen at all. But was he lying just to get under her skin? Or was he telling the truth about it?

And if he was telling the truth, that could be one of the most unsettling facts. Him actually telling her the truth about something. Even if it was about his co-partner in crime that joined up with him because she had an equally weird obsession with Micheal.

She shook her head at how that sounded, as she opened her car door, realizing that she hadn't gotten the list of dates from Vic because of her blow-up at him when she found out about Andrew working for him as a photographer. Because she knew that as a manager, he could juggle other clients as well. So Andrew wouldn't be working on things that are related to Micheal. But just the thought that he had been so close for so long unnerved her so much.

She stared out her car's windshield, thinking about what to do next? Tell Micheal about it or try to keep this to herself and deal with it since essentially Andrew was her problem more than it was Micheal's?

Willow grabbed her phone from her purse before setting it down on the passenger seat beside her, scrolling through the contacts and stopping at Micheal's name. Finger hovering over his name. She wanted to call and tell him, but she didn't want to ruin his day. He was spending time out with Eric and Tommy, going through and checking out art galleries around Los Angeles to pick the perfect one that would serve as bookends to his art tour. Where he would start and also end it when it came time to.

She clicked off her phone and started up her phone. She knew exactly what she was going to do. It was fifty-fifty ongoing to the district office now and checking in on her status at work, especially with how Julie had made it sound when Willow was still in the hospital. She needed to know if she was still eligible to substitute teaching for the district or not. Her phone hadn't rung in a while about and positions that were opened up. Which gave her an uneasy feeling in her stomach that what Julie had rumored hearing about was true.

But maybe that wasn't the case at all. Maybe there haven't been many people out sick in the district lately, she thought.

Knowing that there was a seventy-five percent chance she was just, in fact, overreacting. But there was that twenty-five percent chance that her gut was right and that Julie had told her was, in fact, correct and that her job was in jeopardy after all. And she knew that if she didn't go to the district to find out exactly what was up, then it would eat at her inside.

Pulling up to the parking lot, Willow flipped down her visor mirror to look at her reflection. She wanted to make sure she didn't look too frazzled when she walked into the place. She checked her outfit over jeans and a t-shirt, smoothing her hand over the front of her t-shirt before physically shaking out her body to shake the nerves from her body. Because she could walk into the district office and find out that in fact what she had gone to school for and got a job for could end in a few minutes.

"Don't psych yourself out. It's probably a misunderstanding. Julie must've heard it wrong. You are just going in there to disprove her theory, that's all," Willow said to her reflection, realizing she did almost the same thing on her first day on the job.

She got up and out of her car, flicking her finger on the lock before walking into the building. Immediately she noticed the front office lady, who never would pay any attention to anyone, glanced in Willow's direction and then got on the phone whispering something into the phone as Willow approached.

"Hi, I'm Willow—"

"Yes, the credential personnel person is coming to take you back to her office to talk to you," the older woman said in a neutral tone.

"Oh, so news has gotten around then about everything?"

"No, it's not that. A woman has been coming to her periodically to complain about you. Saying things. And said that she would bring up things at the next board meeting with public comments. I'm sure it's nothing. They just want to talk to you about it," the woman said, possibly to not work Willow up.

Except all Willow could think of would be the one person who would even do this at all. Pam.Willow clenched her hands at her sides, which thankfully because of the high wall the lady didn't see. And just as the lady was opening her mouth to say something else, the door that was off to the side that led to the offices of administrators opened up. And a woman leaned against the door to keep it open, as she looked at Willow with a smile.

"Come right on back, Willow," she said, as Willow walked through the door as the woman closed the door behind them both and walked ahead in the hallway, Willow's heart rate increasing as she felt her head ache. Maybe, just maybe, that twenty-five percent chance from before was going to win out.

Twenty-Eight

Willow threw her keys on the table as soon as she walked into the house. She felt more exhausted than ever after the day she had. So much so that the therapy session that she had scheduled in the afternoon she ended up canceling. Although she knew she would be charged for late cancellation, she talked to the therapist personally, who had suggested that since so much had happened earlier in the morning that it could be useful to vent out her frustrations during the appointment. But Willow insisted on canceling and rescheduling for tomorrow. Since now, with everything, her job was on hold because of the up-rise that had started since she had been in the hospital. Enough time for Pam to talk to other parents at the school and have more parents agree it would be best to not have a teacher working for the district that might have bad people connected to them that could put the kids in danger.

There was the thought that came to mind that they had a point. But it would make more sense if she was actually still together with Andrew, but she wasn't. Willow rubbed her temples as she closed the front door, glancing at the nearby clock that was on the wall that read 2pm.

"Well, it's five o'clock in eastern time," she said aloud as she went to open the fridge just as the back sliding door opened up, making Willow jump as she grabbed for the butcher block full of knives and pulled one out. Turning back around, she was face to face with Larry, Micheal's bodyguard, who had his hands up and a shocked expression on his face.

"Sorry, sorry. Heard a car drive up and just wanted to check and see who it was."

"No, I'm sorry. I'm just on edge. A lot of stressful events this morning," Willow said as she put the knife back into the block and reopened the fridge, grabbing for a beer. Noticing how Larry was looking at the beer in her hand.

"Guess so for you to be drinking at 2pm. You want to talk about it?" He asked as he leaned against the kitchen island, as Willow opened up the fridge and tossed him at water that he caught in the air.

"I guess, since I didn't go to my therapy appointment despite my therapist's wishes for me to come anyway to vent to her," Willow said, taking a big sip of her beer and explained everything from going to the management office and running into Andrew and then having it out with Vic about hiring Andrew. To what happened at the district office.

***

Larry and Willow had moved from standing in the kitchen to sitting at the kitchen table. With Willow sipping at the same beer and finishing it as she set it down on the table and looked over at him.

"So that was my day. What the hell am I supposed to do? Tell Micheal? Wait?"

"What about your psycho ex who tried to kill you both or his ex-wife trying to get you ousted from your job?"

"Both. I just don't know—"

The front door opened, and Willow stopped at the sound of whistling. Hearing keys land on the table. And then Micheal was walking into the kitchen, stopping short at the both of them sitting at the kitchen table.

"I didn't even hear you guys when I came in. How was your day? Get those dates from Vic?" Micheal said as he kissed the top of Willow's head before going off to the fridge to grab a bottle of water.

"Not exactly," Willow said as she looked at Larry, who nodded at her, showing that she should tell Micheal.

"Oh, really? I thought he would be in the office all day? I could call or text him about it," Micheal said as Willow turned around to face Micheal.

"No, it's not that. I saw Vic. We got into a fight and I walked out of the office. It was over the photos again. He was talking about posting them? I can't really remember. That's not what's really bothering me, though. I went to the district office to finally figure out where I stand with them about my future. And they said that a parent had been voicing their concerns about me working at the district because of the incident on-campus when Andrew practically dragged me from the teacher's lounge and into his car," Willow explained, noticing Larry's surprised expression at her not mentioning anything about her run in with Andrew before going to Vic's office.

"Oh, so Pam's been causing trouble. No wonder why I've been getting looks from the teachers and parents when I went to pick him up to drop him off at a friend's house to hangout for a while," Micheal said, going to sit down at the table.

"Oh, that's not all. Apparently, they want me to go to the next district board meeting because parents are coming to voice their concerns along with her. They said they are still thinking about my employment with them," Willow said, getting up and tossing her beer and going to grab another.

"I can talk to her—"

"No, she has been talking since it happened and since we were both in that hospital. You can't say anything that is going to help, especially in the eyes of the district, anyway. It's on Friday. So in the meantime, I just have all the time in the world to be anxious about this."

"Okay. Then I'll go with you, be there for moral support. In the meantime, though, maybe visit the therapist? Talking out your frustrations to a neutral party can be beneficial. As well as there is more than just this district where you can get a job teaching," Micheal said as Larry nodded.

"He has a point. And I'm coming along with," he said, grabbing his phone and texting something on it.

"Just had to clear it with the wife. Passing info earlier rather than later works out better for me," Larry said as his phone dinged, making him smile.

"I'm a go for Friday. Just let me know if you want me to meet you here, drive you there. And my wife hopes and I don't mean this negatively. I'm just quoting her Mr. Stanley. But she hopes that you, Willow, put Pam in her place over this issue." Willow's eyebrows raised at that as Micheal raised his bottle of water.

"Not offended at all. Your wife has a point," he said as Willow laughed, feeling her anxiety about the reality of her future leave her just for a minute.

TWENTY-NINE

The rest of the week came and went for Willow. Spending her time throughout the day worrying about the upcoming board meeting at the district office. She went to see her therapist the following day, after everything happened. And talked it out with her. Letting everything out she felt about the day. Her anger, frustration and disbelief.

And not to her surprise at all, the therapist also questioned, just like Larry did, the fact that Willow didn't tell Micheal about her run-in with Andrew on her way up to Vic's office.

That was still nagging at her. Because deep down, she didn't know herself why she didn't tell him. Either was because she didn't want him worrying, avoiding more drama hitting them both. Or just because she didn't want to bring him back down again when he was just getting ready to get back to normal and launching an art exhibition tour. Which would not help matters if she told Micheal that Vic knew about the Andrew situation and knowingly hired him.

Not yet, at least. Not until after the art tour was done.

Willow checked her reflection in the mirror. And taking her blazer off, walking to the laundry room and throwing it into the dryer. And turning it on to get the wrinkles out of it.

"Ok, that's the second time you've done that. It looked fine before. You must be worried," Micheal said, popping his head into the laundry room, as Willow leaned against the dryer, glancing at him. Taking in his worn jeans and old faded shirt. Both are covered in paint.

"Yes, well can see that I'm more ready than you are for this board meeting. I didn't know you were back painting. I thought your arm and hand—"

"Meeting isn't for a few hours. And my arm wasn't as bad off as they thought. I don't have pain in it like I did when I got out of the hospital anymore. Plus, I need to work on some pieces for them to reproduce for the show," Micheal said, walking into the laundry room.

"Yeah, well, you know that when you are expecting something, time flies. Even when you are anxiously waiting for your career that has barely begun to go up in flames," Willow said, walking past him and into the master bedroom, flopping down on the bed face first in her dress pants and tank top.

"Well, you could take a nap? It might help with the stress," Micheal offered, as he looked down at Willow laying in the bed and saw that her eyes were closed and she was breathing softly. He grabbed a blanket and put it over her before going into the bathroom to take a shower to get ready for the board meeting that was a couple of hours away.

"Ready?" Micheal asked as he parked in one of the parking spots at the school district.

"I don't think I'll ever be ready for this. But I don't want to get in there before it starts," Willow said as she grabbed her phone from her purse, checking the time. But also to distract herself as her heart rate sped up more and more as they waited.

A sudden knock on the driver's side window made both Micheal and Willow jump as Micheal opened up his door, looking out into the darkness at the person.

And Willow couldn't help but imagine it to be Andrew. Because it would be so fitting for him to show up in the most awful time and try to finish what he had started months ago.

But it wasn't as she soon discovered, looking through the dim lighting of the SUV and seeing that it was Larry.

"Why did you do that? You scared the crap out of us," Micheal said, making Larry laugh.

"Hey, if that distracted that one from her nerves over there," Larry nodded towards Willow.

"But also, it looked like they opened up the meeting room so we could go in. I saved us some seats in the back," Larry continued as he stepped back from the door as Micheal undid his seatbelt and looked over at Willow expectantly.

"I'm never going to be ready but hey have to get in there to snag a seat then, don't I?" she said rhetorically, as they both got out of the SUV and walked into the district office. And right into the board meeting room that was off to the side. Going to where Larry had staked out some seats off to the side and in the back. Right next to Amanda, Eric and Tommy.

"You didn't say that you were coming here?" Willow said as she hugged Amanda.

"Hey if I could have you at my performance reviews, I would. But they aren't as public as this. So I thought I would support my best friend in her time of need, especially since someone else is here intent on seeing you crumble right in front of her. And we can't have that at all," Amanda whispered in Willow's ear, making her laugh despite her nerves.

That was, until she turned around to sit and spotted Pam sitting in one chair. And looking right back at her. Her eyes scanned their row and stopped at Micheal before turning back and talking to a woman that was sitting next to her.

Willow sat in her chair, moving her leg from over her other knee and setting it back on the floor. Then back to the other knee. Then both feet back on the ground, tapping her toes against the floor. Anxiously waiting for one of the board members to announce that she was waiting for. Making the meeting almost drag on through the evening, just waiting for the public commentary portion to start. And yet it also seemed to go by quicker than any board meeting that she had ever been to before, which was when she had been in the credential program. And it was a requirement.

But with being on the other side of things, she really didn't want the public commentary portion to be announced. Hoping that against all odds that somehow that would be skipped and they could all just leave.

"You are probably just overthinking this. Watch, she probably won't even go up to that podium at all since you are here. Her angle was to probably blab about this since you weren't around to everyone because she knew it would be back to you eventually making you worried as hell. You just showing up was probably enough to put her in her place. Especially since she does not know what she's even talking about," Amanda said encouragingly as she patted Willow's knee.

"Yeah, you say that, but having the potential that your career is over is intimidating. Especially with the district telling me I had to come to this meeting. I'm sure if I hadn't I would get fired. Hell, even after this, I could get fired. And just when I just started out," Willow whispered back, as the president of the board banged his gavel.

"Now, with that, all agenda items have been addressed. It is time to open up the floor to public comments to the board members about anything concerning the schools in the district. If there are any at this time," the president of the board said as he placed the gavel against the table. His eyes scanned the crowd of people before sitting back in his leather chair.

And there was a pause. Just a second after that announcement, Willow thought Pam was bluffing after all. That she had just showed up to intimidate Willow, just like Amanda had said before. And maybe thought that Willow actually just showing up could be enough to have Pam disregard her plans on following through with talking about the incident to the board.

But low and behold, Pam stood up along with other mothers that joined her up at the podium.

"Hey, you know if you want to get up there and talk. You know I'll be there, standing right beside you in support."

"We all will," Eric added as Tommy nodded, and Willow felt Micheal squeeze her hand, letting her know he was on board with that as well.

"All of us are here today because we want the board to become aware of a teacher. Since it seems like the school in question wasn't going to let me be aware of it," Pam started as she looked out of the corner of her eye at their group off to the left with a smug look on her face before she continued.

"Not even a teacher really, a substitute teacher" she continued, which garnered snickers from her group of moms that were standing up with her in support.

"As if that doesn't mean I'm not a teacher. It's a step in

getting myself out there. I still went through the credentialing to become a teacher. Everyone wants to see that you have some more time teaching under your belt in the hiring process. Hell, not even that though, I have a bachelor's degree. What do her and her little friends have? Huh?" Willow whispered, feeling Micheal's hand squeeze hers again.

"Hey, calm down. You are fine. You are going to still be fine."

"What?" Willow whispered in reply, looking over at him and saw that he looked like he wanted to say something but was stopping himself. And Willow wasn't the only one to pick up on that.

"Oh no, you can't be seriously siding with her," Amanda hissed at Micheal, leaning closer to Willow so she could whisper quieter. Willow looked around and saw that people weren't looking up at Pam and her group of mom friends, but at their group now. Making Willow's heartbeat even faster at the unnecessary attention that was being placed on their group.

"Stop it," Willow said as she put her hand on Amanda's shoulder, pulling Amanda's focus from Micheal back to her.

"It's not that at all. And you know that," she whispered. "You know he isn't siding with her. It's because that is Evan's mom. Everything that is happening affects his relationship or could with Evan. I don't want you guys fighting about this when it's my situation to deal with. Hell if it has to come to it I'll walk out here right now, screw the job and just apply to other districts to avoid all this drama," Willow said quickly before she turned her attention to those standing in front of the podium addressing the board members.

"As she said, this is a substitute teacher that is causing problems. While working she caused a rather startling display that caused many of the kids some trauma," another woman who was standing next to Pam added. Willow narrowed her eyes, trying to place this woman. Her hair and voice were familiar. She had to be a parent at the school.

Which would make sense because the few times that she had subbed at the school, Willow would only see the parents if their kids were taking their time collecting their things from the classroom. And they would have to come in to collect them so Willow could lock up the classroom. But something about the woman was more than familiar to her. More than just a passing incident or exchange of niceties before.

"I caused the startling display? Really? And classes were in session before Andrew even came on campus. He went into the break room, which is attached to the front office. It wasn't like he found me in the classroom and dragged me through the halls. It wasn't like it was recess or lunch when this happened," Willow whispered, more to herself because she couldn't believe what she was hearing. And out of the corner of her eye, she saw Amanda nod her head in affirmation about the events that took place.

"Well, you might as well come up here, since it seems you have another side to the story. What was your name again? Willow?" Pam said, raising her voice so everyone could hear her. As more faces turned in Willow's direction. And she noticed more familiar faces from Evan's school in the crowd, teachers that she had seen.

"when all you are spouting is lies, as if you were even there when it happened, what do you expect her to do as you rake her over the coals in front of everyone," a voice piped up, as the person stood up from their seat. It was Julie.

Pam looked Julie up and down and then looked over at Willow with a smile. One that would look sincere and nice to anyone else. But it was reeking of hate.

"Maybe we should put an end to this, I can see that this is going to become a debate and this isn't the place for this," the president of the board said just as Pam had stepped up to the podium again, the smugness wiped off her face at the sudden abruptness of change as the President of the board banged the gavel.

Majority of people got up and started filing out of the room, many looking over at Pam with narrowed eyes. And Willow didn't know if those were other teachers from other schools or other parents that wanted to address things to the board that didn't have time to because of the switch in atmosphere that Pam and her group of moms brought to the meeting.

"Come on, let's get going so we don't have to run into anyone," Amanda said as she patted Willow's knee as they and everyone else in the group got up and left the boardroom and walked out of the district office. Willow stopped just as she was about to get in the car, her brain nagging at her to go back and talk to the board members.

She turned on her heel and opened up the door, just as Pam was walking out of the building. Willow moved to the side as Pam bumped into her. And not accidentally, as if to knock Willow off her footing. And Willow simply moved further to the side, not looking Pam in the eye as she continued back into the district office and into the boardroom where the board members were wrapping things up and getting ready to leave themselves.

"Hi, I don't know if you know. I'm the teacher that is or was the subject of the commentary tonight and I wanted to apologize for that. I was told by one staffer that I had to come to the meeting and make my presence known," Willow said as she walked up to the table. And just seeing how the board members exchanged looks between each other before the President spoke up.

"Yes, that was what we told them. We've become aware of the situation when more people start talking. Which I guess was that parent and her friends from that school. We talked to staff at the school and got the details about it and know that there were slight exaggerations when it came to the events. And you know that we back our teachers when certain instances occur," he said, and Willow noticed it looked like he was looking beyond her.

"I'm sensing a but coming but also I'm getting the feeling that someone could've paid you off," Willow said, knowing that the districts usually support their teachers, but this conversation felt like it was taking a turn.

"Are you implying that we would take bribes to sway our decision-making?" The president said, in a sharp tone as she felt the conversation's tone shift now.

"I'm just saying I know that mom and I know—" she said as the President looked her directly in the eye.

"We were considering letting you work but now, there will be a discussion on where to place you if at all, you will hear from us through a phone or email in about a week's time," he said, as he collected his notes and put them in a folder and got up. Clarifying that he was done talking to her.

Willow looked down at her hands and saw that they were shaking with the realization that she was the one that ended her career with the utterance of the exchange of money. When she knew Pam could've done that right after everyone left the room. She turned on her heel, leaving the room and trying to take deep breaths as she bumped into someone. She looked up, expecting it to be Pam looking at her smugly after the exchange, but it was Julie.

"Hey," Julie said simply before taking Willow in for a hug as Willow's emotions that she had been holding back bursted forward. Shaking in Julie's arms as Julie pulled back, rubbing her fingers under Willow's eyes.

"Hey, I know this is hard but I might have some news that

could dry those tears for you," Julie said as Willow took a breath, a shaky one as she tried to stop crying.

"And what's that? You know another district that would be willing to hire me?"

"Not exactly, but I know a lieu pole to still work for this one. I have a friend that works for the after-school program. They aren't technically a part of the district, but through another program entirely. And they are always looking for people to work mornings and evenings for the kids that come to stay at the program. I could pass along your info to them. I know you would be a perfect fit. And that schedule kind of lends you time to go back to school and get your master's like I know you want to," Julie said as Willow felt the tears come up again from her eyes as she grabbed Julie and hugged her.

"And just went I thought I was going to have a huge meltdown,"

"Hey, it's not a guarantee, but you know you can put me down as a reference. I'll forward your info to them and they'll probably be sending you an official application through their website," Julie said, patting Willow's back before pulling away.

"Thank you,"

"Oh, it's no problem. I want to see that smug look come off that face of her. Thinking she can fabricate things to get her way," Julie said with a smile as Willow looked off in the distance and saw in the parking lot that Micheal was waiting by the car. Julie turned to look at what she was looking at with a smile on her face as she looked back at Willow.

"I won't delay you anymore. I just wanted to give you the news so you wouldn't feel so awful for the rest of the evening," Julie said as Willow nodded, hugging her once again.

"I can't thank you enough really," she said to Julie before pulling away.

"Oh really? It's no problem. But if I was hearing the things correctly? But I heard you are going on tour with that man across the country. I require and the other teachers require some photos on your social media so we can live vicariously through you," Julie said with a smile, making Willow laugh as she nodded.

"Oh definitely I will," Willow said as she walked off to the waiting SUV, seeing Micheal waiting for you.

"Where's Larry?"

"Left with the others in their car. He thought we would want time alone," Micheal said as walked around and opened the passenger side door for Willow as he went around and got into the driver's side.

"So you went back and talked. How was it? Good or bad. I saw you crying but I couldn't gauge if that was good or bad tears," Micheal questioned, starting up the truck but not shifting it into gear as he waited for her answer.

"About that tour. You still think you can fit me on the itinerary?" She questioned.

THIRTY

A Couple Months Later...

Willow sat in a chair, scrolling on her phone through her social media, as her phone dinged. Getting another notification of a like on one of her photos that she had posted only yesterday. It was or her and Micheal

She was putting her phone back in her pocket when it vibrated. She looked at the notification and saw that she was getting a call. From Eric.

"Hey what's up?"

"What do you mean, what's up? Is he ready? I mean, I don't think there would be that much for him to prepare,"

"Oh, I didn't know someone officially hired me on as staff," Willow joked, as she heard the exasperated sigh on the other line.

"I'm here with the owners and based on the schedule, isn't he supposed to be out by now?"

"Well, I don't have it in front of me, but don't you deal with the stuff manager?"

"Willow know I'm not HIS manager, I'm more Vic's assistant manager that deals with stuff on the road,"

"Ok, so then you should be the one-" she was saying as the door that she had been sitting in front of opened up. Revealing Micheal. He was wearing his usually black t-shirt and black pants, and he was giving Willow that smile that made her infectiously want to smile right back at him.

"Hey, you know you don't have to wait out here. Come in," he said, moving over to the side and opening up the door more so Willow could come in.

"Hey, I'll let Willow know," Willow said on the phone as she clicked off the call, ending it just as she heard Eric talking on the other end.

"Eric?"

"Yes, he's wondering where you are. Apparently someone is running behind schedule," Willow said, tapping on Micheal's chest, as she walked into the room. Which was just a backroom that the art gallery had provided for Micheal to have for his personal use before and after the art showing.

"Ah, so that's why you were waiting outside and not in here with me," Micheal said from behind her as she took in the little room and saw the vanity that had been put up for him. Next to a rack where he could put his clothes on and change into the ones that someone else on the team had set out for him to change into. And looking at the mirror she saw that Micheal had set up a couple photos. One from the Laughlin trip of the entire group Amanda had taken on her phone. Another was of Evan. And the last one was of Willow and Micheal together. One one that she had taken on her phone a couple days ago and had posted on her social media.

"When did you have time to check my social media, or even have it printed out?" Willow said as she grabbed the photo to look at it closer. It was an off-day on their travel schedule. Micheal had specifically had days on the travel days so it wasn't back-to-back gallery showings across the country. Which meant more time to spend together and exploring the cities. It was of them together, standing in front of the iconic Las Vegas sign before going to the hotel that night.

"You know, after we are done here, we are walking around the Las Vegas Strip, right?" Willow asked rhetorically as she put the photo back up on the mirror before turning around to face him.

"Oh, I knew you were going to say that. There are a couple places I do want to take you," Micheal said as he turned to face her, his clothes in hand that he had come in wearing.

"Hey, I can do that. I think Eric really wants you out there. Your public awaits," Willow said, taking the bundle of clothes from him as he smiled and kissed the side of her face before grabbing for his jacket that he put on over his t-shirt. She hung up his clothes on the rack. Coming over, spinning him to face the mirror as she stood behind him, fixing his jacket. She smoothed it out with her hands and fixed the lapels.

"Ok, I think you are good to go," she said, holding out her hand as he put his phone in her palm. Just as there was a knock on the other side of the door, startling them both.

"Hey, come on, lovebirds. This is why I said no going into the dressing room," Eric said as Willow laughed immediately. Her dream from months ago sprang to her memory about the same thing. Funny how dreams emulate life, or rather predict it.

"I was just helping him fix his jacket," Willow said, hearing the sigh from the other side of the door.

"Yeah, yeah of course you were," Eric said as Micheal opened up the door as Eric mockingly shielded his eyes from them before laughing.

"Come on, let's go," Eric said, moving so Micheal could lead the way, as they both walked out of the makeshift dressing room and further out into the hallway.

"Have fun," Willow said as Micheal smiled.

"Oh I will, but I'm definitely looking forward to the after part to all this," Micheal said, leaning down to kiss her before parting and looking over at a smiling Eric.

"What?" they both asked in unison as Eric just looked at them, but Willow noticed he stared at Micheal a bit longer before clapping his hands together.

"Nothing, nothing. It's just nice seeing you two so happy, and Willow are going to have to tell me what you have planned after this," Eric said as they started walking out of the hallway and out into the main exhibition area. Willow stopped to wait in the hallway, next to a chair next that was just out of sight. She had been to enough of these that she didn't feel the need to go out with him, since it was Micheal's exhibition. As her phone vibrated and she took it out of her pocket and looked at the notification, seeing that Amanda had texted her.

That was their routine. Either calling to check up on each other or texting, since Amanda couldn't come along because of her job. Willow started texting away as the sound of the crowd that had been waiting for Michael cheered at his arrival, and she looked around the corner, seeing him standing with Eric, who was off to the side. As Tommy was near the front, the camera clicked away. And Micheal was all smiles.

Her phone dinged again, thinking it was a text from Amanda. She looked down and saw that it was an email notification about the application that she had put in a week after that dreaded board meeting. Looking down at her phone and then back up, smiling. Willow had never thought that a couple months ago she would be here but couldn't be happier with how her life had twisted and turned to get her here.

After the art exhibition, Willow walked hand-in-hand with Micheal to a waiting car that was in the back parking lot that would take them back to their hotel room that was a couple blocks away.

They walked up to the blacked out SUV, Micheal opening the door for the both of them, as Willow did a double-take at who was sitting in the backseat already. Eric and Tommy were sitting there as Eric patted the seat next to him.

"Come sit next to me, Micheal go sit next to the driver," Eric said as Willow looked up at Michael who just rolled his eyes as Willow got in next to Eric, door closing behind her as Micheal got into the front passenger side seat without question.

"I'm so glad we have a couple days off," Tommy said as the car started going, and Willow leaned her head against the window of the SUV, trying to stifle a yawn.

"No kidding. I've finally had a ringside seat to this. Who would've thought there is so much that goes into it?"

"Hey, I just showed up where I'm required to. It's those two that do most of the work," Micheal said from his seat as he leaned back and turned to face them all.

"Yeah, well, we stay up late. Sleep in until 9am. Rinse and repeat for a couple months out of the year," Eric said as he had his phone out texting away.

"You look pretty tired, maybe we should just go straight to the hotel room instead of going out," Micheal commented as Willow shook her head, blinking as the car stopped at a light. She had been splitting her attention between the conversation and trying to not fall asleep in the car that she hadn't realized that the already short drive from the art gallery was over within a blink of an eye.

"No, no, I'm fine. I just want to change first, that's all."

"Ok," Micheal said, but Willow noted he didn't sound too convinced about that, as they all exited the SUV and entered the hotel, each of them going in separate directions towards the elevators since their rooms all weren't on the same level.

"Come on, let's get you up to the room," Micheal said as he wrapped his arm around Willow's waist as they got into an elevator and up to their floor walking the short walk to their room.

Inserting the keycard it clicked open, as Willow surged forward past Micheal, landing face first into the plush hotel bed with a tired sigh.

"Yep, definitely knew you weren't going to come out tonight," Micheal replied with a laugh.

"Give me five minutes," Willow said in a muffled voice, since her face was still on the bedding.

"How about you stay in? Catch up on sleep. I know this constant schedule is something to get used to. I can stay as well."

"No, no. You haven't had time with just them. Go out. Have fun. Call me if anything comes up. And don't do anything I wouldn't do," Willow said, moving her face from the bedding. There was a bit of her that was disappointed in being so exhausted and she didn't want to drag down the rest of them. And he was right. She could use the time to get more rest from adjusting to the grueling schedule they were on.

"I'll call if anything fun comes to mind," Micheal said, leaning down to kiss the side of her face and then her lips, lingering more before pulling away from her.

"Have a good night,"

"You too," Willow replied, feeling her eyes droop as she heard the door open and click.

Willow woke up to the sound of her cell phone ringing, as she fumbled to try to grab it before it went to voicemail..

"Hello?" Willow says, yawning.

"Hey, we were out and thought that you would wanna come along. Change into something nice because it's a nice place that we are going out to eat." Micheal said as Willow was questioning what hour it was that he was calling her, from where, and if he was drunk.

"Ok, I guess. Give me a couple of minutes." Willow said, as she hung up the phone. Getting up and going through her suitcase, picking out one of the nicer dresses that she had packed for this kind of spontaneous outing, a nice black body-con dress that hugged her curves in just the right places and a pair of heels since Willow had not had time to wear them yet. Willow was straightening out the mess that was her curly hair when there was a knock at the door.

"It's open!" Willow shouted from the bathroom, as she saw Tommy and Eric walk in.

"Come on, Willow, everyone is waiting! Let's go!" Eric said, as Willow did a last pass through her hair, turning to look at them as they looked Willow up and down as if checking to see if what she was wearing was right.

"I think that's good. You think that's good?" Eric asked Tommy, as he nodded.

"Yeah, plus everyone is waiting. Come on!" he said, as they took Willow by each arm.

"What's the rush, guys? I don't think anyone would put a reservation for something around... 6am! It's 6am!" Willow said, as she got a glance at Eric's watch on his wrist.

"You've been out since 5am with Micheal?" Willow asked as all they did in response was smile at her, as they led her through the maze that was the hotel, and pushed her in a black suburban. Closing the door behind Willow and hitting the back as it took off without them.

"WHAT THE HELL?" Willow questioned, as she looked at the driver, who was just straight-faced, looking ahead.

"Don't try to get any information out of me miss, all I know is the address of where I'm supposed to be dropping you off at." He explained, as Willow sat back in the seat.

Willow was sitting watching the suburban drive through the desert. Thinking that this is exactly how horror movies start or even true crime stories. Which she probably shouldn't have watched in the hotel before going to sleep earlier. The driver turned off the main road into a beautiful housing development that was just off the water. Once it stopped, the driver got out and opened the door for Willow.

"They said that you should walk down that path," he said as Willow looked out and saw a sand pathway that followed. With the help of the string lights that lit the path before it opened up into the main area. Willow felt her throat tighten as she tried to keep from crying at the sight before her.

Eric, Tommy and Micheal, all wearing suits. And Amanda standing in-between Eric and Tommy wearing a dress and heels. And looking like she was barely holding it together herself. And Micheal got down on one knee.

"I've been wanting to ask you for days. This ring has been burning a hole in my pocket. I've been carrying it ever since the accident. I just didn't know when the right time was. Until we saw a gap in the schedule. Willow..." he said.

"And here I thought you were joking when you said that you made impulsive decisions before,"

"This isn't impulsive. Well, kind of is, but we had the time and I didn't want to finish this exhibition without asking you. Will you marry me, Willow? I know we've been through a lot of crap together, but I wouldn't have it any other way," Micheal asked.

"Yes," Willow said as she watched him place it on her ring finger as he stood to his full height to kiss Willow.

Willow hugged Micheal and saw that Eric, Tommy and Amanda's attention was no longer on them and further off into the distance. And she felt Micheal stiffen in her arms. Hearing the crunching of the sand on the path as footsteps came closer to their group.

ACKNOWLEDGMENTS

Paige and Michelle, my gal pals. You guys really supported me through the writing process as I was working on this sequel and helped me smile through the hard days of writing.

To my mom Shelly, I have to thank you for helping me buckle down when I felt overwhelmed with the workload on having to work on the book with getting closer and closer to the deadline. It really helped me motivated into getting this book completed.

Thank you to my alpha/beta reader Kate Stone. You were awesome and very helpful during the early parts of the writing. I found you randomly off social media and it really helped early on with your messages about getting a connection with my main character Willow with her struggling with anxiety.

And to my readers, old ones that started out reading my first novel when it was published last year and the new ones that are just getting to reading this series after this second book has launched. Or even those that are just getting to this series later on. I love you all and appreciate you. Every new person that takes the chance on reading my work. I thank you and I can't express how much that touches me that you would take the time to read my works. And I can't wait to see what comes off this whole writing career in the future. (Especially for the sequel to this story!)

About the Author

Jessica Danielle lives in California with her two dogs, Zoey and Stella. She is an avid watcher of true crime programs and a listener of true crime podcasts. And is a lover of Classic Rock Music. This is her second book.

twitter.com/Jessica50481448

instagram.com/jessica_danielle__

tiktok.com/@jessica_danielle__

amazon.com/Jessica-Danielle/e/B08YKGXG7L?
ref_=dbs_p_ebk_r00_abau_000000